FALLEN

Alyssa Rabil

About the Author

Alyssa has always had a love for fiction. She read her first romance novel from her mother's collection. Her first love story was about a tiger that fell in love with a zebra. Alyssa lives in the Wild West with her cats and her family. She loves cooking and writing.

FALLEN

Alyssa Rabil

BELLA
BOOKS

2023

Bella Books, Inc.
P.O. Box 10543
Tallahassee, FL 32302

Printed in the United States of America on acid-free paper.

First Edition - 2023

Editor: Ann Roberts
Cover Designer: Kayla Mancuso

ISBN: 978-1-64247-458-9

PUBLISHER'S NOTE

Acknowledgments

Many thanks to all who made this book possible, to Ann Roberts for editing and Bella Books for publishing. Thank you to my family for always believing in my dreams. Most of all, thank you to Schmom and Tarper. You are my lighthouses. Thank you for never leaving me to drown in stormy seas.

CHAPTER ONE

Ava is convulsing.

Faith's bleeding out.

Andy's shaking like a leaf and she's so mad she's not sure who she's going to yell at first when they finally come around. Why the fuck didn't they tell her where they were going? Why didn't they wait for her to get to town?

Faith called her about an hour ago, shouted a few directions and then the line went dead. At least she had the sense to call.

Now, Andy's got a dead angel outside and she's going to have to burn and bury it on her own. She can't have the body getting reanimated by something else. Its wings are massive. That's going to be a problem. The wings usually disappear.

Andy goes to her little sister first. Faith's pulse is steady, and the wound isn't as bad as the blood makes it look. She checks Faith's head—no bumps or injuries. It's got to be a spell, but that's just a guess. She's not the doctor in the family, no, that's Dr. Faith fucking Black, who is currently passed out on the floor of this godforsaken shack. It looks like the blood isn't Faith's.

That means blood loss isn't the problem like Andy had first suspected.

"Fucking monsters." Andy's talking to herself. It keeps her calm. She shouldn't even be here.

She checks Ava, her aunt on her father's side. No external injuries, but her eyes keep rolling back in her head and she's drooling.

"Ava!" Andy shouts and gets no reply. This has magic written all over it. When she's done in here, she's going to chop that angel into one hundred pieces and mount the wings on a wall. She's got a nice assortment of individual feathers from her kills over the years, but these wings—big, glistening, and inky black—will be the star of her collection.

She hears a groan behind her and turns to see Faith blinking and clutching her forehead. Andy runs to her side, anger replaced with relief. "What happened?"

Faith takes a minute to orient herself. "Ambush," she answers. She spots Ava and scrambles to her feet. She crouches next to her and rolls her onto her side. "Jesus, Andy," she growls. "Priorities. Ava could choke to death like this."

Andy is unmoved. "What happened?" She hates repeating herself.

Ava stops shaking and Faith holds her fingers against her wrist to check her pulse. "We were ambushed by another trapper. Thought we had the drop on the guy. Don't know how he knew we were coming. The angel might have warned him." She brushes her long hair out of her face and looks up at Andy. "Can they do that? Can they sense humans?"

Andy nods, waiting for more information.

"Knew it," mutters Faith. "Ava owes me twenty bucks."

"If she wakes up," snaps Andy. She shouldn't snap. It's been two years since she's talked to Faith in person. This isn't how she wanted their reunion to go.

"The guy hit us with tranquilizer darts. She'll come around in a minute."

Andy jerks her head to the door of the shack. "I figured the angel got her."

Faith perks up. "Angel? She's still here?"

"Yeah, it's outside. Didn't you kill it?"

"She's dead?" Faith looks like she did when their dad told her there was no such thing as Santa Claus. She doesn't give Andy a chance to answer. "Stay with Ava, I'll be right back." She gets up, moving entirely too fast for someone who was just unconscious a second ago, and goes outside.

Ava's breathing is back to normal and her eyes are shut. She's still and appears to be sleeping.

"Andy!" her sister is shouting from outside. Andy is on her feet and out the door in a flash. Old habits die hard. She freezes when she sees Faith.

Her pain-in-the-ass, dickhead, stubborn baby sister has hoisted the blood-soaked angel into a sitting position and is trying to lift it all by herself. "Can you push her wings into place?" Faith grunts the question as she shifts the creature's body.

"Just leave it," says Andy. "I'll hack it up and burn it once—"

"No!" Faith shouts. She looks angry, then horrified. She finally settles on an expression somewhere between kicked puppy and guilty toddler. "She's not dead."

Instinct and muscle memory take over and Andy's got her bowie knife in her hand. Faith drops the angel on the ground and stands over it to prevent Andy from slitting its throat.

"What the hell?" They don't have time to do this right now. Andy needs to act while the thing can't fight back.

The shuffle of boots on gravel distracts both sisters. Ava's up and coming outside. She's rubbing her head and has her other hand pressed against the side of the shack to support herself. "I told you not to call her," says Ava.

"I thought we were dying," snaps Faith.

"Well, you thought wrong, Doc," says Ava.

Andy takes advantage of their engagement and lunges for the angel. She underestimates Faith's reflexes. Andy's on her back and Faith's working to disarm her. She succeeds and pins Andy to the ground.

Jeremy Black taught his daughters well. If he were here, Andy's sure he'd be proud to see Faith hasn't forgotten her training.

Andy shakes her head. She can't think about her dead dad right now.

"Andy," Faith says her name like a warning, "I need you to be calm. I've got some things I need to explain, but first, I need you to help me get the angel in the van." She releases Andy slowly, probably hesitant, not knowing what Andy will do next.

Andy glares but nods. She's curious now. It's not Faith's fault she's keeping secrets, the Black family is genetically predisposed to lie.

"We parked about a quarter of a mile down the road," says Ava. "Can you two behave long enough for me to go get it?"

Faith looks at Andy.

"I'll be good," says Andy.

Ava leaves to bring their van up to the shack. They don't speak while they wait for Ava. They've got a lot of shit to talk about but now just isn't the time.

Instead, Andy starts a mental list of questions to ask Faith. She'll bring them up once they're back at Ava's ranch and everybody's got a drink in their hand. Faith had a lot of explaining to do *before* this shit show happened, and now Andy figures interrogating her will take the rest of the evening.

When Ava pulls up, Andy rolls her eyes. Of all the cars at Ava's disposal, their ride is an ugly two-ton monstrosity of a creeper van. It's white and only has front windows. Faith slides the door open and instructs Andy on the best way to situate the angel. Andy doesn't need instructions. She knows how to handle possessed bodies. She shoves the angel's wings in place and Faith snaps, "Be careful."

Andy rolls her eyes but tries to be gentler with the other wing. She's dismembered enough of these to know which parts go where. Their training shaped them. Faith's a damn good doctor with a great marriage and an almost normal life. Andy's just a psychopath.

Andy grips the large bone near the shoulder and, following Faith's orders, carefully encourages the rest of the wing to fold at the joint. The angel twitches and Andy checks to make sure it's still unconscious.

It has possessed a woman with dark hair who looks to be somewhere in her late 30s to early 40s. Andy makes sure to absorb her features so she can see if someone's got a missing persons report out for the body. The human is beyond saving, and there's nothing Andy can do if she left behind a grieving family. Still, Andy likes to know. It's a habit she picked up from her father.

Now isn't the time to think about that shit, though. It's never the time. She focuses on the wing, and only then does she notice how badly both wings are damaged. They're crusted with blood and pale skin peeks through where patches of feathers are missing. Andy stops pulling on the joint and runs her fingers down the length of the massive bone. It's fractured in two places.

"Broken wing," she says.

"Great," mutters Faith. She pushes Andy aside and inspects it. Andy surrenders to her sister's medical expertise. Faith sets the wing and gently folds it in place.

Andy doesn't ask why she's bothering to be so careful with a monster. She's sure it's a hell of a story. She keeps her mouth shut while they load the creature and secure it. Andy deserves a fucking medal for how patient she's being.

They're thirty minutes away from Ava's. Andy tails behind them in her truck. Faith drives like she's ninety. Andy grips the wheel a little tighter and curses under her breath.

They reach the ranch forty-five minutes later and Andy is again silent and obedient as they unload the angel. They set it down on a gurney that Ava apparently had waiting, then Faith turns to her.

"The cabins are clean." Faith points across the lawn to a row of three guest cabins. "Pick one."

Ava built them years ago when the ranch was a ranch instead of ground control for monster killers.

"Is that your way of telling me to beat it?" asks Andy, crossing her arms.

Faith sighs and suddenly looks ten years older. "Please. We'll meet you over there in an hour."

Andy bites her bottom lip and eyes her sister in a futile attempt to decode her. She fails, and surrenders. "Fine. See you in an hour." She turns on her heels and goes to sulk in one of the cabins.

When she first found out what Faith did for a living, Andy pitched a massive fit. Angels and demons come from a dimension parallel to the human world. There's a rip somewhere in the fabric between the worlds. Humans can't find it, but monsters seem to know how to exploit it.

In theory there's a war going on in the other dimension and the monsters come to the human world to get away. At least, that's the lore Jeremy passed down to his daughters.

Angels and demons blend in for the most part and generally people don't notice them. In fact, very few people know they exist. However, every now and then, someone spots something weird flying around. That's where Andy comes in.

They can't sustain their true forms here, so they possess humans—pose as people and prey on their life force.

It's Andy's job to know this shit. It's her job to see the signs and kill the poor bastard the monster's possessing. It's impossible to save someone after possession.

Andy's seen more than one occasion where a creature left the human alive, but the human still retained some of the creature's power—almost like they were still tied together. It drives the victims mad. Possession means death. No exceptions.

That is, unless you're Dr. Faith Black and Dr. Tristan Naser, and now apparently Ava Black. Faith and Tristan started a rehab facility in Oregon where they try to heal and help people after possession. They claim it works.

Andy's just waiting for the inevitable day when Faith realizes their work has been an exercise in futility. If people could be saved, Jeremy would have found a way to save their mother. If people could be saved, Andy might be able to save her still. She can't afford to think like that. Hope gets people killed. She takes another drink.

Andy and Faith were trained to trap and kill. They come from a long line of trappers on both sides of the family. It wasn't unusual for trappers to marry each other. That life didn't allow for outsiders.

Trappers were part of an ill-funded federal program, one that technically didn't exist. Kids weren't supposed to grow up as killing machines, but it wasn't uncommon in their line of work. Andy and Faith weren't the first children to learn how to vivisect an angel before they learned to drive.

She gives Faith and Ava half an hour to get comfortable before she sneaks back up to the main house. The door's locked because Ava is the master of keeping secrets. It doesn't matter. This isn't the first time she's been locked out of the house. It takes her three tries to guess the right code for the garage. The large metal door rumbles and groans as it slides up against the ceiling. Andy slips in and makes sure it shuts behind her. She'd be worried about the noise, but most of the rooms in the main house are soundproof. Ava relies on surveillance cams and her bizarrely accurate sixth sense to alert her to danger.

Andy's pretty sure they took the angel down to the chop shop (lovingly named for the angels and demons that have been dismembered there) in the sublevel of the house. Last time Andy was down there she was a teenager.

She gets into the house via the door connecting the kitchen to the garage. She creeps through the halls trying not to think about how long it's been since she's been inside. Faith was sixteen when she put her foot down and refused to go back with her family. Andy had just finished packing her duffel into the truck when she heard Jeremy and Ava shouting. Faith had been standing behind Ava, cheeks burning red and tears in her eyes, but the way she was staring at Jeremy... It was like she'd decided her father was the devil incarnate.

Jeremy and Andy left without Faith. That was about twenty years ago. Ava gave them regular updates and the four of them would meet up on the road every now and then, but Jeremy never went back to the ranch. Faith went to med school. Ava and Andy went to her graduation. Jeremy showed up for dinner but didn't stay long. As far as Andy knew, that was the last time Faith saw their father.

Andy rubs a hand over her face. This place always has this effect on her. It's always like coming back to a home she was never allowed to want. She finds the basement and is careful going down the stairs. She can't remember which ones creak. Once she's finally down in the dark, musty underbelly of the house, she hears a door slam and Ava lets out a string of obscenities.

"That little bitch bit me," says Ava. She sounds shocked, pissed, and downright offended.

"I told you not to touch her," says Faith.

Ava mutters something back in response.

Andy sneaks closer until she can see them standing in the pale fluorescent light outside of the entrance to the chop shop. A heavy-looking metal door and seven locks secure the room. Clearly Ava has done some upgrades.

"I thought she'd be angrier," says Faith.

"At least she's talking to us," grumbles Ava. Faith's tending to her hand. "We'll need to get Tristan down here to check out her mental state."

Faith laughs. "I think we know her mental state."

Andy rolls her eyes. They're wasting time. There's no reason to delve into the angel's mind. They need to kill it and be done.

"I'm trying to be serious," says Ava. "She's been through a lot since your daddy died. Hell, she'd been through a lot before that. You both have."

Andy frowns. They're talking about her and not the angel.

"I know," says Faith. She lets out her breath in a puff. "I shouldn't have left them."

Ava yanks her hand back and finishes wrapping the gauze on her own. "What'd I tell you about thinking like that? It's survivor's guilt. You got out and you're better off for it. Jeremy didn't do Andy any favors. Not that she's broken. She's still pretty hardy."

Faith nods. "I know. She's strong. I just worry about her."

Ava puts a hand on Faith's shoulder. "You can stop worrying. We've got her back. It was my mistake letting her go the first time, not yours. I'd be a fool to let her wander off again."

After a moment of silence, Faith says, "She's going to hate me when she finds out."

Ava rolls her eyes. "News flash. Andy's not capable of hating you. It's going to take her a while to understand, but she will. Hell, you convinced me, didn't you?"

Faith nods and seems to feel better.

Andy feels a stab of guilt for not being the one to comfort her sister. How many times in the past has Faith needed a friend and Andy's not been there for her? How many times has Faith been upset and Andy didn't know because she was too far away, or too busy to pick up her phone?

Andy pulls a flask from her pocket and takes a nice, deep pull. Whiskey can't heal, but it sure as hell helps the pain. It's her own fault Faith doesn't feel comfortable talking to her. Andy's an abrasive, stubborn, monster-killing, son of a bitch. Faith's a compassionate, fearless, healer.

Suddenly, something crashes into the door of the chop shop from the inside.

Faith looks to the door, then looks to Ava. Andy decides to come out from hiding.

Faith sees her first. "I told you to wait."

"I did wait," says Andy.

"It hasn't been an hour," says Faith, glancing at her watch. "How long have you been standing there?"

"Long enough to know you two need help," answers Andy.

"As much as I hate to admit it," says Ava, "you're right. We could use your help on this one."

"We don't need help," says Faith.

Ava shakes her head. "You know humans but your sister knows angels. We're not going to get anywhere unless we can figure out a way to talk to this one."

"Is it mute or something?" asks Andy.

Faith raises an eyebrow. "No. Angels can't speak in human form, and I don't know their language well enough to write to it."

Andy rolls her eyes. It's like amateur hour. Monsters can speak, most choose not to around humans. "So, you want me to get in there and kill the angel, but save the human?"

"It's a little more complicated than that," says Faith slowly. "I don't think that's a human."

"Not right now it isn't," says Andy. She knows Faith is already feeling vulnerable. She should be nicer. She *should* be a lot of things she isn't.

"It's a hybrid," says Ava, apparently tired of pussyfooting around the issue. "There's not a human to save and there's no angel hiding under that skin. We're looking at something I've never seen before, and frankly, didn't think was possible."

"But," says Andy, "you don't know for sure because you can't talk to it."

"Bingo."

"Why do you think it's a hybrid?"

She's heard rumors of otherworldly beings mating with humans to create something new. But she's never seen it before and figured it was just a tall tale designed to keep trappers hypervigilant.

"Her powers are weaker than they should be," says Faith, "even though she's injured. And when we found her, she had… She was in bad shape. Her wings were…" She chokes again so Ava takes over.

"Somebody captured her," says Ava. "I think she was a pet or something." The disgust is obvious in her voice. "They had her caged. We found a journal with her with all kinds of records from blood tests and x-rays and physical exams. We're pretty sure she's at least partially human."

"And," says Faith, "her wings don't disappear. So, either she's something new or she's a hybrid."

"Hybrids are a myth," says Andy.

"Actually," begins Faith, and Andy just hates it when her sister gets that tone, "genetically speaking it is possible; it's just not common."

Andy's too tired for this shit and her brain's too busy trying to keep her memories at bay. She shrugs. "Okay then. What do you want me to do?"

"She's restrained," says Faith. "We were hoping you could go in and see if you can figure out a way to communicate with her. She's pretty freaked out, but I think she's stopped throwing things. I really need to check on her wounds or I don't think she's going to last much longer."

"Fine," says Andy. "But if I do this, I do it alone."

"No—" Faith protests.

"Deal," Ava says. "But you can't kill her and you can't hurt her. You've got to trust your sister on this one."

"Whatever. I'll be back in a second."

She goes to her car and retrieves a Kevlar vest, her bowie knife, a handgun, and a bottle full of the concoction her dad called "holy water." It's basically acid, but Andy can't remember how exactly he created it. She's got the recipe somewhere. She spilled some on her boots once. The liquid hissed, bubbled, then ate through the leather before Andy had a chance to get her foot out. She ended up with third-degree burns and she's still got the scar.

Sufficiently armored up, she returns to the chop shop. Faith is obviously reluctant, but she lets Andy go in alone and shuts the door behind her. The first thing Andy realizes is that the chop shop is no longer a chop shop—it's a goddamn recovery room.

Andy rolls her eyes. If Jeremy knew about this, he'd never let Ava live it down. They used to come here to dissect and dispose of creatures, not host them like it's a B&B. There's a bed instead of a table. The walls are covered in pictures and charts instead of knives. The water hose is a makeshift shower and there's even a stall for the toilet. Andy snorts. The term "creature comforts" has never been truer.

The angel is sitting on the back corner of the bed, withdrawn, and tucked against the wall with its wings pulled forward around its shoulders. It looks submissive, but the wings twitch and give it away. It's prepared to attack and defend. It's in bad shape, but Andy can't afford to underestimate it. She approaches slowly.

"Those two knuckleheads outside think you can't talk," says Andy. She pulls a small notebook and a pen out of her pocket and scribbles something down in Enochian, the language of monsters. Andy is by no means fluent in the language, but she knows enough to get by. "I know better. I've heard your kind speak before."

The angel's eyes are a deep, dark brown, and they follow Andy's every move.

"What do you call yourself?" asks Andy.

The angel doesn't answer.

Andy approaches the bed slowly. She can see the angel's restrained to the bed frame. She sets the note down in front of it. "You don't have to answer. A little bird tells me you're part-human, part-angel, so for now, you can just be Monster."

As Andy backs away, the angel lunges and that's exactly what she was hoping would happen. She gets her knife out first. If the angel attacks her, she can kill it, claim self-defense and Faith won't be able to say jack shit about it.

Turns out, the angel must have broken free of its restraints after Faith and Ava left, because the chains aren't attached to the bed anymore. It tackles Andy to the ground, and she can tell it's using every ounce of strength it has left to try and kill her.

It knocks the knife from her hand but fails to do much more. It's much stronger than it looked when she first saw it, but in the end it's not enough.

Andy delivers a few well-placed right hooks and the angel crumples.

It lands on its broken wing and hisses in pain. It starts to push itself back up and manages to get up on its knees, but it's too weak. It's bleeding, bruised, and exhausted. It stares at the floor while Andy reaches for her gun.

Bullets can't kill an angel in its real form, but when they're bound to a body, they're vulnerable. This thing isn't human, not according to Faith. Andy can shoot it and not have to worry about the residual guilt of taking an innocent life.

Andy stalks around to stand in front of the creature. Its wings hang down, uncomfortably bent with its body so low on the floor. It takes several deep breaths, then slowly raises its head to meet Andy's gaze.

Her hand itches on the trigger, but Andy can't bring herself to shoot. Something about the fucking look the angel is giving her throws her off. It lost the fight. It knows it lost and it's ashamed. It knows it can't win and it's just ready for this to be over. It's tired, broken, and defeated on a level Andy isn't sure she understands. Then again, maybe she does. Maybe that's why she doesn't kill it.

It's staring at her. Its eyes are too human. They don't glow and they aren't an otherworldly color. They're just deep and pleading.

She lowers the gun and backs away from the angel. She can't look into those eyes anymore. They're hopeless and Andy's own hopelessness is reflected in them. She grabs her knife from the floor, makes sure her other weapons are secure, then hurries out of the room.

Faith is on her the minute she emerges. "Well?"

"That thing has death wish," says Andy. "Best thing you can do is put it out of its misery." She doesn't know why she says that. It's not like *she* had the courage to kill it.

Faith starts to pry, but Andy doesn't want to talk right now—can't talk right now. She leaves without another word and retreats to her cabin where a bottle of liquor is waiting for her.

CHAPTER TWO

An unfamiliar number keeps calling her father's phone without leaving a message. She notices the number the second time it rings. Whoever it is, has called twice since she's been at Ava's.

After a few hours someone knocks on her door. She's not surprised to see Faith. They both know they need to talk, and Faith must know Andy deserves an explanation.

She vaguely remembers Faith and Ava discussing Andy's well-being earlier. Faith probably called her shrink husband, Tristan, and asked for advice on handling her miserable big sister.

Andy shouldn't be bitter. Faith's just trying to help. Hell, that she even wants to help after all these years might mean their relationship is in better shape than Andy suspected. She leans against the doorframe. She's made all these assumptions before Faith's even had the chance to speak.

Faith rubs the back of her neck, and she can't seem to hold eye contact with Andy for very long. "We uh…" she begins, "we need your help."

Andy nods. "Let me grab my gun." Even buzzed she has the skills to kill an angel. She could probably do it three sheets to the wind, blindfolded, with one hand tied behind her back. Maybe if she drinks more, she'll be able to follow through this time.

But Faith shakes her head and stops her. "No, we—she—we think she's trying to talk to us."

"For fuck's sake, Faith," Andy grumbles, "I told you the best thing you can do is just let it die."

"She wrote us a note." She digs a sheet of paper out of her pocket and shows it to Andy.

Andy recognizes it as the note she left on the angel's bed earlier. In Enochian, she'd asked the angel for its name. Beneath her question is the angel's Enochian reply.

If you will not kill me, then let me go.

"I know you're already more involved than you want to be, but she's not talking to us. I need to treat her injuries. We've had her for about a week and she hasn't tried to communicate until now. It would mean…It would mean a lot if you'd help me."

Andy's eyes snap up from the paper to Faith.

Her face is already pale. She must know her mistake.

"A week?" barks Andy. "You've had that fucker for a week? I thought you just found it."

"I can explain," says Faith.

"You've been promising to explain since I found you this afternoon and so far, I've gotten zip for an answer."

"It's hard to tell you—"

"Bullshit. You don't *want* to tell me."

At that, Faith leans in, fists clenched. "It's hard to tell you because you don't listen. I know you'll get pissed before you even try to understand, and this"—she points to the main house—"means a lot to me. This is my life, Andy. I know you're not happy with it. I know I'm an embarrassment to you and your trigger-happy drinking buddies. I know you love me because I'm blood but hate me because of what I do. I know I'm a disappointment to the family name. You don't have to like it, or approve of it, but don't get mad at me if I don't confide in you."

Faith's red in the face when she finishes her rant. She's still posturing. Still looming.

Andy could easily step forward and back her down—respond to the challenge and use Faith's respect for her big sister against her—but she doesn't.

Faith has clearly been holding that in for a while and Andy suspects more than half of that was meant for Jeremy, but he's dead and the next best thing is Andy. That thought sickens her a little. She never wanted to be like her father.

She takes another pull of whiskey and looks away from Faith. She knows a normal, functional, well-adjusted human being would say something comforting right now. She knows she has as much explaining to do as Faith does. She knows she should put the liquor down and hug her sister and tell her she's so fucking proud because Faith got out—because Faith had the courage to break away from their fucked-up little family—because Faith made a life for herself and she's healthy and happy and she found love in a loveless world.

Andy's so proud of her. Faith's smart and brave and passionate and a million other things Andy isn't.

When another gulp of liquor burns down her throat, she realizes why she really came back. She came back for Faith.

And Faith's still looking at her. She's relaxed a little, but Andy can feel her eyes trying to see into her—trying to figure out what Andy's thinking. Andy owes her. Jeremy died owing her. Somebody needs to tell Faith she's still a Black, still a member of the family.

Finally, Andy realizes that's the real challenge here. Faith's daring Andy to validate Faith's status as the family disgrace.

Andy sets the bottle down at her feet, takes a step forward and puts a hand on Faith's shoulder. Her sister's scowl deepens and her jaw clenches. She's ready to fight.

"Faith," Andy begins, "you're the best of us. You always have been."

Faith suddenly shrinks back to eight years old, and her face relaxes. God—is that really all it takes? Could this have been fixed years ago with just a few words?

I'm an asshole.

"Dad and I…" Andy's voice falters a bit. "We're so proud of you. You were never an embarrassment. You're all the things I never could be." Feelings, confessions, tears of atonement, these are not things Andy does. But she'll do anything for Faith.

Andy doesn't get to say more because Faith has her trapped in a suffocating hug. Faith's shaking, Andy's shaking. They're both in tears and maybe everything isn't perfect, but it's better.

Andy pulls away first.

Faith's shoulders are hunched and she's peering, bleary-eyed, through her bangs. "You know," she says quietly, "when you and Dad left, I quit talking for about a week. Ava was great, but I was still adjusting, you know?"

Andy nods.

"I was so lost, but then…I guess you guys had just finished another job killing a demon and you called me." Faith gives her a little half-smile.

Andy knows this is going to break her heart.

"As soon as I heard you—knew you weren't gone forever—I was fine." Faith's voice cracks. "For a while I lived off those calls and I'd track you guys to figure out when I could see you again." She laughs. "I had a map." She's tearing up again.

"I'm sorry, Faith." It's not enough. "I should have stayed with you. I let Dad come between us. I'm so fucking sorry. You have no idea how much I regret—"

"Yeah, I do. I bet you regret leaving as much as I regret staying."

"You were right to stay. You didn't miss anything. Dad's drinking got worse and his temper got shorter. By the time we went out on that last job, Dad was too fucked-up to fight it and I…I couldn't save him." Andy's not ready to tell that story.

Faith knows some of it. Andy called her the night it happened—drunk, because like father, like daughter—and gave her the rundown. Jeremy found the demon. He fought. It won. It got away. Andy left out the gory details. She left out the part where she'd failed their father.

Faith must know Andy's not comfortable saying more

because she slaps her on the shoulder and offers the family's trademark bury-your-feelings grin. "Will you talk to the angel?"

Andy will do anything Faith asks. "Yes, but you've got to tell me the whole story. I need to know what I'm dealing with."

Faith explains most of it on the way up to the house. When they get down to the basement, Ava helps fill in the gaps in the story.

It was by accident that they found the angel. Ava got a call from another trapper saying something weird was going down on a farm outside of Tacoma. The trapper said he was too far away to check it out but figured Ava would know who to dispatch.

Ava took the case herself. Faith and Tristan met her in Yakima. They suspected it was a case of madness brought on by possession. People were hearing noises, seeing strange lights, and every now and then the earth around the area would quake slightly.

Sometimes humans gain special powers after the monster leaves them. The powers usually kill them if someone else doesn't do it first. Faith says they got to the farm and found the angel caged inside a modified grain silo. Faith stops the story there and looks to Ava for help.

"She was in bad shape," says Ava. "But she was pissed. We knocked her out and had to keep her drugged the whole way home. She's still in bad shape. Won't let us get close long enough to finish treatment and we can't keep drugging her or her heart might give out."

"How did you guys end up in the shack?" asks Andy, though she suspects she already knows the answer.

Faith sighs. "I thought, if she could stretch her wings, maybe see the sun, she'd feel better."

Ava shoots her a look.

Faith shrugs. "I wanted her to feel free. I thought it would help her trust me. So, this morning, I let her go outside."

"Instead," says Ava, an I-told-you-so tone coloring her voice, "as soon as Faith got the angel outside, she broke free and flew off."

Andy just shakes her head. "So, you weren't ambushed?"

"No," says Ava. "She wasn't strong enough to fly fast. We followed her until she crashed. We figured she tired herself out during the flight."

"She's strong, though," says Faith. "We hit her with a few tranq darts, but she fired back with a spell and knocked us both out."

"I knew you weren't tranquilized!" shouts Andy. She should have trusted her gut. She knows magic when she sees it.

"Yeah, well." Faith shrugs. "You know the rest of the story from there." She nods to the door of the chop shop. "We need you to tell her we're trying to help and let her know I want to treat her injuries. Without treatment, I don't know how long she's going to last. I did what I could while she was out, but she hurt herself again when she escaped."

Andy doesn't give a shit how long the angel lasts, but that's not the real issue here. This is a chance for Andy to prove she respects Faith and respects what she does. Faith's trusting her and acknowledging Andy's expertise. Andy needs to do the same. If Faith says the angel is worth saving, then the angel is worth saving.

Andy sighs and rolls her shoulders. "Ready when you are."

The angel is on the floor with its head bowed. It doesn't look up when Andy enters. Faith has coached her, told her to be calm and respectful. Why Faith thinks the angel isn't going to lash out again as soon as it gets the chance, Andy doesn't know. Angels have nothing but contempt for the beings of this world. There may have been a time when a few good angels tried to protect mankind. According to the history, their deeds are the source of the various religious myths and legends.

Trappers know better. There is no Heaven. There is no Hell. There is no God. The creatures of the other realm only bleed into the world of humanity to feed and wreak havoc.

Human energy sustains their powers.

Andy looks at the hybrid on the floor. She didn't think it was possible for the monsters to breed with humans. This has all the signs of a new problem. She plants her feet and crosses her arms.

After an extended silence, the angel raises its head and examines Andy. Its eyes are electric, but they are the only feature of its body that show any sign of stamina. It's dying.

It makes a sound like it's clearing its throat, and much to Andy's surprise, it speaks. "Oriana." Its voice is hoarse, strained from disuse.

Andy unfolds her arms and moves in closer. "What?" She's not sure if she's hearing English or Enochian.

"My name. My name is Oriana."

"Okay."

The angel looks back at the floor. "I am ready."

"For what?"

"The execution."

"I'm not here to kill you. My sister is outside. She's a doctor. She wants to treat you. I'm here to tell you to let her help."

The angel's head sinks lower.

"It's your own fault they sent me. You should have talked to the other two. They're the ones who are trying to save you."

"But you are their warrior."

"No, I'm just the most willing to kill you."

"Will is what separates warriors from those they defend."

Andy rolls her eyes. "Look," she says, pointing to the door, "those idiots aren't going to leave me alone until I talk you into letting them help. However, I'm willing to make a deal."

The angel looks up and Andy doesn't miss the way its wings shift. She has its full attention.

"If," begins Andy, "you let them clean you up, feed you, and you give yourself some time to heal—if after all that, you still want to die, I'll gladly be the one to do it."

The angel frowns. "What does that mean in terms of a time frame?"

"Two weeks. You've made it this long, two more weeks won't kill you and if it does"—she shrugs—"problem solved."

"I must spend two weeks under the care of the doctor and her companion and if I still wish to die and am unable to do the task on my own, I may call upon you and you will assist. Is that correct?" The angel is frowning, but it doesn't seem unhappy with the deal.

"Yeah."

"What do you gain from this?"

"I get to kill you without pissing off the doctor."

"You had the opportunity to kill me earlier. I attacked. You were defending yourself. Surely your doctor would have understood."

"Yeah, well, I fucked up. I should've pulled the trigger, but I didn't. I can't change that so we're both stuck with plan B."

The angel gives Andy a slow, contemplative nod. "Two weeks," it mutters.

"Deal?"

"I'm not sure I have much choice in the matter, but yes, we seem to have reached an agreement."

"So, you're not going to throw a fit when the doctor comes in?"

The angel scowls. "I will obey your orders for two weeks. If you do not want me to resist, I will not resist."

"Close enough." She takes a few steps back and bangs on the door to signal Faith.

Both she and Ava enter the room. They're each carrying a med kit.

Faith looks directly at the angel. "May we approach?"

The angel nods.

"Use your words, monster," says Andy.

Faith shoots her a nasty look.

Andy holds up her hands. "Sorry. Use your words, *Oriana*."

Faith looks stunned. "You got her name?" She turns to the angel. "Oriana? That's your name?"

"Yes," answers the angel.

Faith sets her kit down. "My name is Faith Black. This is Ava Black. It's nice to meet you."

"The human in the corner said you are a doctor," says the angel.

Faith shoots Andy another look. "You didn't introduce yourself?"

"Sorry, forgot." She leans around Faith but doesn't step closer. "I'm Andy."

"Andy Black," finishes Faith. "She's my older sister. Ava is our aunt."

"Do I belong to all of you now?" asks the angel. "Or just the one who knows Enochian?"

"We don't own you," says Faith. "We're going to fix you and let you go home."

The angel's lips tighten, and it dips its head. "You can fix me. I won't resist."

"Thank you," says Faith. She starts pulling stuff out of her kit and Andy can tell it's killing her not to ask too many questions.

Ava breaks first. "So, you're half-angel, half-human?"

"Yes."

"How...er...what...I didn't think that was possible," Faith says.

Oriana just looks at her.

Andy rolls her eyes. "Clearly it's possible." She turns to the creature. "Faith wants details. She wants to know how you work. She's a big nerd like that."

Oriana seems to understand. "Giving birth to me killed my mother. I suppose our respective species are not meant to breed. Perhaps, once my two weeks here are over, you could dissect me and inspect my body for your studies."

Andy shakes her head, motioning for Oriana to stop talking, but the damage is done. Faith and Ava don't miss a beat.

"What's she talking about?" asks Ava. "What's this about two weeks?"

They're all looking at Andy and she doesn't know how she can put this delicately.

Oriana seems to get the message. "If I do not survive treatment, of course."

"Why'd you say two weeks?" asks Faith.

"Your sister said that was my estimated recovery time."

Thank the Lord it came up with a cover story. Faith would never approve of their deal.

"That's a good estimate," says Faith. "You should heal pretty quickly. I guarantee you'll survive. You have my word." She and Ava are back to focusing on the monster. "But don't get discouraged if it takes longer before you're totally back to normal."

"I won't get discouraged."

Faith points to the open shower area. "I'd like to get the blood off you. Then I can get a better look at your injuries."

"All right."

"Do you need help?" asks Faith.

Andy answers, "Yeah. It can't stand by itself."

"I can manage," says Oriana.

"*Managing* to do something and *successfully* doing something are two different things."

Oriana looks to the ground. "I won't resist your help."

Faith glares at Andy, but Andy's not sure what she did wrong. She can tell she fucked something up, though, because the angel isn't making eye contact anymore.

Andy settles on distracting her. She steps up to whisper to Faith, "Angels aren't big on having humans touch their wings."

"But I have to touch them."

"I know, just thought you should have a heads-up. It's kind of a personal thing."

Faith nods and turns to Oriana. "I need to inspect your wings and bind the one that is broken. I'll be gentle. You can tell me to stop at any time."

"I understand."

Ava and Faith approach with caution. Faith stays true to her word and inspects the wings carefully and quickly. The three women help the angel bathe. At first, Andy doesn't volunteer to help, but Ava and Faith drag her in. Andy ends up soggy, with soap and feathers clinging to her.

She doesn't help with the medical crap. Faith has it down to an art and Ava makes a damn good nurse. The whole thing takes about two hours. When they're done, Andy's surprised by the improvement.

Oriana seems surprised as well. Its broken wing is wrapped and set. It tests its mobility within the bandages. Satisfied, it flexes the other wing. The movement seems to reassure it.

"Better?" asks Faith.

"Yes," answers Oriana. "Thank you."

"Good." Faith shoots a sideways glance to Ava before continuing, "I know you're not comfortable around humans. We can't begin to imagine what you've been through, but we'd like for you to feel comfortable here." She licks her lips nervously. "I'm sure you don't want to stay in the recovery room, but we don't want you to escape again."

Oriana looks to Andy, then back to Faith. "I won't attempt to escape."

"We've made up a room for you upstairs," says Ava.

"We've also got cabins," says Faith. "Ava and I like the house but Andy likes the cabins. You're welcome to stay with her."

Andy rolls her eyes. "Yeah," she says, "by all means, crash with me."

She's not trying to be an asshole, but how much does Faith think she can change in a day? She's not going to hurt the angel because Faith asked her not to. But it's still a monster and Andy's still a killer.

Oriana cocks her head to the side and looks to Andy. "This is my choice?"

"Of course," answers Faith.

Oriana is still looking to Andy, which means Ava and Faith look to Andy as well. Oriana is waiting for an answer. Ava and Faith are daring her to fuck this up.

"Of course," echoes Andy. "Stay wherever you're comfortable."

Oriana frowns and its good wing arches slightly.

Andy's seen that look before.

It's preparing to defend itself. "I would like to stay in the house."

"Great," says Faith. "I'll show you your room. Are you hungry, or do you want to rest? There are several rooms that are free. I guess it depends on which view you'd like the most."

While Faith babbles, the angel keeps its focus on Andy. It has relaxed its good wing, but it's still frowning. Maybe it's still pissed about being alive or maybe it's confused. Either way, it's not saying anything to Faith about it.

Andy sighs. "Ladies, can we have a second?"

Ava scowls. "You want us to leave you two alone?"

"Yes. Please."

"Don't hurt her," warns Faith.

"I won't. I just want to talk."

Faith turns to the angel. "If she hurts you, scream, okay?"

The angel nods.

Ava claps Andy on the shoulder as she leaves and whispers to her, "Good luck."

Andy starts to ask what the fuck that's supposed to mean, but Ava's already gone. Faith backs out of the room slowly and pulls the door closed.

Andy steps closer to the angel. Its good wing droops submissively. Andy stops. "Why were you staring at me?"

The angel's eyes dart to the ground and it hangs its head.

"Hello?" Andy tries again. "You looked like you wanted to say something. What's going on?"

"You are a trapper."

"Yeah."

It's still looking at the floor. "I do not understand this place."

Andy suddenly feels like she's in over her head. Is this thing upset? Does it need a hug? Fuck. Faith should be in here, not Andy.

"You are my new master," it says, voice lower. "Unless you have been tasked with returning me to my old master."

"I'm not your master." She finds herself moving closer to the angel and stops. "And I'm not returning you. Ava and Faith would skin me alive if I took you back."

The angel looks up, scowling. It's watching Andy with those piercing eyes and for the first time, Andy lets herself really look at it.

Oriana is clearly malnourished. Her ribs jut out beneath her skin and her shoulders are too angular. The borrowed pants she's wearing from Faith are barely hanging around her hips and the T-shirt doesn't fit much better. Then again, that could be because of the way they cut the back of it for her wings.

Andy finally realizes she's not looking at a creature inhabiting a human. She's looking at the actual creature.

Everything about this rubs her the wrong way. She should have killed it when she had the chance. She should kill it now. She shouldn't be wondering what the creature is thinking and feeling. Oriana is a monster—a thing—nothing more. But this thing is Faith's project and Andy must behave.

"Look," Andy begins, "I'm not the best one to talk to about this, whatever is happening right now. Faith and Ava are the people you want."

"They would conceal the truth so as not to frighten me," says Oriana. "They care. You do not. You will tell me the truth."

"I can't argue with that. What truth are you looking for?"

"What is my status here?"

"You're Faith's patient."

"I am not owned?"

"No, you're free, I guess."

The angel snorts. "I am not free. If I were free, I would be able to leave. If I were free, your sister and your aunt would not have brought me back here after I escaped. If I were free, I would be allowed to die on my own terms."

Andy shrugs. "I guess you're not *completely* free."

"Then I am a prisoner."

"You're not a prisoner."

"Then let me go."

"We covered this already. Two weeks. That's it."

"Then you will kill me."

"*If* you still want to die, then yes; I'll kill you."

"If I want to live?"

"Then Faith and Ava will probably let you go."

"Where I will be killed or captured by my master, you, or someone like you."

"What do you want me to say? You don't want to stay here, you don't want to go back, you're not sure if you want to die… What the hell are you looking for?"

The angel hangs its head again. Its good wing curls slightly around its shoulder. Andy doesn't know what that means. She backs away. When she feels the door behind her, she knocks.

Faith opens it immediately.

"We're done. She's all yours. I'm going to sleep." She leaves before Faith can question her. She knows that's the wrong move to make. She nudges Ava on the way out. "That thing needs help."

She hurries out of the house, across the lawn and down to her cabin. When she arrives, she locks the door behind her, and then collapses on the bed. She's done with this day.

CHAPTER THREE

Andy avoids the house as much as she can over the next few days. Faith asks her what she said to the angel. Andy tells her—or at least tries to. She's not sure what it wanted or how to explain. Faith seems to understand, though. Tristan arrives on a red-eye flight and Andy greets him briefly outside.

Andy's only had passing impressions of Tristan. He's usually quiet. Faith has always said he prefers to observe rather than participate. He's not difficult to avoid. He seems to love Faith which means Andy is going to have to get to know him better eventually. Not now though. She has too many things on her mind at the moment.

Almost a week goes by. Andy can't sleep. Every time she closes her eyes, she sees Oriana asking to be free. She sees the faces of other angels she's killed. She sees her father. She tries to remember her mother. She spends a few hours tossing beneath the blankets. It's cold in the cabin but she doesn't use the fireplace. The days bleed together.

It's another night. She's sitting on the porch with a drink in her hand when she sees Faith walking across the lawn.

"Shouldn't you be asleep?" asks Andy.

Faith sits down beside her on the porch steps. She's gearing up for something, Andy can tell.

"Did Ava send you out to check on me?" asks Andy. She knows she's been irritable. She knows her eyes are sunken and bloodshot. She knows she's been avoiding people.

"Tristan and I are leaving tomorrow."

Did I scare them away? Are they leaving because of me? Did the angel die?

"Oh."

Faith looks at her through her bangs. "We got a call today about a possession. We need to take care of it sooner rather than later." She pauses. "Tristan wants to talk to us before we go."

"Why?"

Faith bites her lip. She was clearly elected to be the one to retrieve Andy from her self-imposed isolation. She's not here by choice. "We're worried—well, Tristan and Ava are worried." She extends her hand for Andy's glass.

Andy gives it to her and Faith drains it.

"I had someone to talk to when Dad died. Tristan talked me through it, made sure I had my head straight. Ava came to visit. You didn't have anybody."

"It's been a month. I'm fine."

"A month isn't long enough to get over someone that important. I didn't care about him nearly as much as you did and I'm still dealing with the fallout."

"I don't want to talk about it. There's nothing to talk about even if I did."

"I'm not going to push you. I just want you to know you're not alone."

But Andy will be alone. As soon as Faith and Tristan get on that plane tomorrow, Andy will be alone. Of course, she has Ava, but Andy won't stay at Ava's. She'll leave soon. She knows herself well enough to know that. Andy doesn't know where she'll go after this. She tells herself she'll pick up where her father left off. She'll kill the monsters that invade her world.

She tells herself things will go back to normal. She tells herself she's still a fighter even if Jeremy is dead.

Faith lightly punches Andy in the shoulder. "You going to take us to the airport tomorrow?"

"Yeah. What time?"

"Got to be there by seven a.m."

Andy grumbles.

Faith rolls her eyes. "Don't be such a butt."

It's a childhood taunt. It's an insult from a time when Andy was old enough to curse but Faith wasn't. Jeremy didn't have many rules, but age-restricted cussing was one of them. Andy grins. It's been years since they've dared to tease each other.

Faith smiles back at her. "You better be there tomorrow."

"I'll be there."

Faith goes back to the house and Andy goes back to the cabin and begins packing her things.

They arrive at the airport at 6:30 a.m. because Andy drives too fast. Ava said her goodbyes at the house and stayed behind to watch the angel. Andy parks and walks Faith and Tristan inside instead of dropping them off at the curb. They say goodbye in a corner away from the security line.

Tristan hugs Andy and gives her a quick peck on the cheek. "Faith said she talked to you," he whispers. "You can call me any time for any reason."

Andy laughs to suppress whatever other emotions are trying to claw their way to the surface. "Thanks. You might regret that offer."

Faith's up next. She crushes Andy in a tight hug. "Ava said you packed your duffel. Planning on heading out?"

Andy struggles free of the hug so she can answer. "Yeah. I need to hit the road."

Faith nods. "We figured. That's why we hid your stuff."

"You what?"

"Ava will give it back later."

"What about my gear?"

"She'll give it back later. I think she doesn't want you to go."

"Damn it, Faith, I know that was your idea."

Faith doesn't even pretend to be sorry. She just shrugs. "Take care of Oriana for me. Ava's not exactly a master of conversation." A little frown pulls at the corners of her mouth. "And, Andy? Stop calling Oriana *it*. She's not a thing."

Andy lets out an indignant huff as Faith and Tristan head to security. She goes back to her truck and checks the bed where she's sure she'd locked her bag last night. It's empty. A pathetic, secret part of her is glad she must stay. Technically, she could leave anyway. She could get new gear. She could buy new clothes. She doesn't own much. This is a thinly veiled excuse, but it's an excuse, nonetheless.

Andy stops to restock her cabin before heading back because *everything* she owned was in the truck and Faith left no stone unturned. It's a testament to how distracted she is that she didn't notice things were missing.

It's still early when she gets back. Ava's on the porch of the main house when she pulls into the driveway. Andy unloads the truck and reluctantly decides to be social. She sits in a rocker beside her aunt.

"Don't get too comfortable," says Ava.

"Why?"

She jerks her head toward the house. "Oriana wants to talk to you."

Great.

Andy rolls her eyes. "Is it urgent?"

"She says no, but she's been itching about something for the past three days. Tristan tried to talk to her, but she'll only tell him so much." Ava smirks. "Looks like you've made a friend."

Andy mutters under her breath. She gets up and forces herself to go into the house. She gets out her flask and takes a long pull before going too far. She can hear someone upstairs. She finds the angel's door ajar and raps her knuckles against the wood.

"Come in," says Oriana.

"Ava said you wanted to talk to me." Andy leans against the doorframe, flask still in her hand.

"I want to know if our deal still stands. You left abruptly the last time we spoke, and Faith said you are beginning to feel differently about my kind."

Andy sighs and closes the door.

"First of all," begins Andy, "I don't feel any different toward creatures like you. Second, our deal is still on as far as I'm concerned."

Oriana nods. "Tristan, Faith, and Ava do not know. They are happy with my progress. When the time comes, I will make an attempt on your life. You will kill me defending yourself. This will ensure your sister does not get angry with you, as requested."

Andy's not sure she's ever met something so desperate to die. Suddenly, a memory of an angel begging while Jeremy demanded information flashes across her mind. Andy feels dizzy. She takes a step back and braces herself against the wall.

Oriana is on its—*her*—feet, good wing twitching. She's studying Andy. "You're not going to be able to do it, are you?"

Andy takes another drink, draining the flask. "I can do it." She pushes herself from the wall and leaves, pulling the door shut behind her.

She composes herself before going back out to Ava. She makes an excuse; she's tired from getting up early, she didn't sleep well last night. She retreats to her cabin, pours another glass of whiskey and crashes into bed. Finally, sleep comes.

CHAPTER FOUR

The only one in the house is Ava. One human will be easier to bypass.

Oriana waits until well into the night before she leaves her room. These humans do not keep her locked in. They seem to mean it as a gesture of trust and goodwill. Oriana knows in exchange for this gesture she is supposed to offer her trust.

She scowls as she creeps silently through the house. She will not give her trust in trade for the lack of a cage.

Oriana steps outside and stretches her neck to greet the moonlight. A cool breeze rustles through her feathers and for a brief, blissful moment, she forgets she's broken. She forgets she is an unholy, inhuman mongrel. She is a small girl clinging to her father's hand before gathering the courage to take her first flight.

She sucks in a deep breath and buries the memory as air fills her lungs. The good memories are hers and no one can take them from her. They are her only possessions, her secret well of hope.

She stretches her good wing and flexes the other as best she can. She takes a running start and throws all her strength into getting airborne.

Her flight is short-lived. She crashes in a heap in the gravel driveway. The pain is blinding and she's not sure if she screams. She pounds her fist into the ground and grits her teeth. She pushes herself back onto her feet and stands. She can do this.

She extends her good wing. Then she moves the broken one and a new, spectacular jolt of pain shocks her body. She crumples to the ground, panting. She is too weak to escape. She is always too weak to escape. She stares at the gravel beneath her fingers. She crashed many times when she was a girl. Her father always knew how to inspire her to try again, always knew what to say to make her stand back up.

Oriana does not call upon those words now. She does not let those memories surface. If someone senses her joy, they will find a way to take it from her.

A voice calls out to her in the darkness, low and secret. "You hurt?"

Oriana flinches. She did not even notice Andy approaching until she spoke. She pulls her extended wing back to her side and for a moment, considers running. She does a quick assessment of her odds of success, then decides against it. She's failed again. She's trapped here. Death is the only escape. She is at the trapper's mercy.

Andy mutters something, but Oriana isn't sure what she says. Suddenly Andy's arm is around her waist as she pulls Oriana to her feet and leads them back to her cabin.

Dr. Black and Ms. Black were kind to her after her first attempt to escape. They are not here now. She's alone with Andy. Logically, the only way to stop Oriana from trying to escape is to punish her.

Though Andy has changed, Oriana knows she still has a job to do. Warriors are enlisted to do the unsavory deeds others cannot stomach. Oriana decides she cannot begrudge Andy for whatever happens next.

Oriana's father was a warrior. She swallows the memory. She isn't sure how she will be punished for her insubordination. She begins to mentally prepare herself, shutting down her thoughts and entombing herself in her mind.

Andy pauses as they enter the cabin. She huffs, then leads Oriana over to her bed.

Oriana focuses on the gentle hum of an appliance coming from somewhere off to the right, a refrigerator? It doesn't matter. She listens as the noise becomes a metronome and she begins to let herself drift away.

Suddenly something touches her cheek. Oriana isn't ready yet. She needs more time to shield herself from whatever is about to happen. She's still too alert, too vulnerable. She jumps and pushes herself back across the bed. In her haste, she pins her broken wing and cries out. The pain is too intense, but she knows more will follow to rectify her behavior. She must get herself under control. It hasn't been this difficult for her to refocus her mind since she was a child.

She searches the room wildly, desperate for anything that will help her enter the trance she needs to survive. She sees Andy, who says something. She has one hand raised slightly, but she lowers it as she steps back.

A hand. That's what touched her. It was Andy's hand. *Why* Andy's hand touched her is still unclear. She obviously didn't intend to strike her. Has Oriana really lived without pain long enough that she is beginning to fear it again? How long did it take her to build up that indifference? Five years? Ten? How long did it take that fortress to crack and allow fear to ooze back in? Weeks?

Oriana pulls her knees to her chest and covers her head with her arms. The humiliation is almost punishment enough. She is weak. She has always been weak. She was born as the embodiment of weakness. She was the weakness that killed her mother. She was the weakness that killed her father. Now she is alone, weakness waiting to infect someone else. She almost feels obligated to warn Andy.

Andy clears her throat. "Mind if I sit down?" she asks.

It's Andy's bed. She doesn't need to ask Oriana's permission. The question reeks of some polite human custom.

Oriana nods. She wonders, briefly, if her mother would have been able to teach her the ways of humanity, if she could have helped her fit in. She stomps the thought down quickly.

The bed sinks as Andy takes a seat. "I brought this," she says.

Oriana does not want to know what Andy brought from wherever she went.

"Can I—" begins Andy.

Oriana can sense that Andy's heart rate has increased, and her scent is different. Is it fear? Does Andy fear her?

Oriana lifts her head to peer at Andy. She tries to regain some semblance of control.

"You okay?" She's holding a damp cloth in her hand. She sounds genuine.

Oriana nods. She allows herself to relax back into her body. Her face is hot and her eyes sting. There is little she can do to conceal her feelings now. She has never been able to hide shame. "I'm sorry," she says. She overreacted. Andy was trying to help.

"I thought you might have a fever," mutters Andy. "I didn't mean to—ah—startle you, I guess." She extends the cloth. "This is cold, but it might help. I mean, it'll help if your face feels hot, otherwise it'll just be cold."

Oriana's face is hot. Andy seems to be treading lightly now. Oriana is so broken and pathetic that she's managed to elicit pity.

I am broken. The acceptance of that fact does not sting as much as she thought it would. *I am so broken I cannot differentiate kindness from cruelty.*

"I shouldn't have jumped," says Oriana. "I'm sorry."

"It's okay. I scared you. I shouldn't..."

Oriana hangs her head once again, heavy with humiliation. Of course, Andy saw her fear. One benefit to angelic power is Oriana's ability to detect minor changes in a human body. She can hear Andy's heart beating furiously. She seems to be panicked about something, but Oriana cannot begin to fathom what that could be.

"I wouldn't trust me either," says Andy at last.

Oriana isn't sure what to make of that statement. If Andy does not want her trust, what does she want? Oriana sighs and decides to begin with the cloth, because obviously Andy wants her to take it. Andy mentioned something about her face, so Oriana lifts the cloth to her cheek. It is mercifully cool. She closes her eyes and feels a modicum of tension ebb away.

Movement on the bed startles her and she opens her eyes. It was a trap, a diversion. Andy has moved and her hand is raised. Oriana braces herself for the pain and searches for a weapon. But Andy is still unarmed. She's staring at Oriana and her hand is trembling. Is it a greeting? Is Andy greeting her as a human would greet another human?

Oriana slowly lifts her hand. Andy's heart is pounding. Oriana's hearing is not as sensitive as it would be if she was a pure angel, but it is more sensitive than a human's. There are some advantages to her mutant genome.

She touches the tips of her fingers to Andy's and Andy's cheeks begin to blossom in a pink that quickly becomes red. Oriana has no idea what to make of that. She's never seen that kind of reaction from a human. Perhaps she did something wrong. Perhaps Andy does not know her skin is turning colors.

"Your face is red."

Andy jumps, snatches her hand away and stumbles away from the bed. She turns again to face Oriana. Her breathing pattern has changed again, and her heartbeat has increased to a rate Oriana thinks could be unhealthy.

Oriana frowns. "I'm sorry."

Andy just stares at her for several seconds, making no note of the apology. "We should sleep," she says. Her voice is strange, forced.

"I will return to the house," says Oriana.

Andy shakes her head. "Stay put. I'll crash on the couch."

Her tone is not commanding. She cannot possibly want Oriana to stay. She seems terrified. "I shouldn't stay."

"Well, I don't want to wake up Ava trying to get you back inside, so you're kind of out of options. If Ava wakes up, she's going to want to know what you were doing outside, and you'll have to explain."

That is a fragile protest. "I make you uneasy."

Andy shakes her head. "You're staying. We can make each other uneasy together."

Oriana has no skills to navigate this kind of interaction. It seems they've entered some kind of negotiation. She takes a guess and hopes it is acceptably human. "I will stay," she says, "but I will not take your bed."

Andy points to her wings. "Those won't fit on the couch."

Oriana stops herself from rolling her eyes because Andy seems to be aiming for kindness. "I'm aware."

"You can't make them…you know…" Andy seems to be talking about her wings. "They don't disappear?"

"No."

"Then how are you going to fit on the couch?"

"I will sleep on the floor."

Andy sighs. "You can't sleep on the floor, Oriana. Ava would skin me alive if I let you do that."

There's that phrase again. Andy seems to be constantly worried that she will be "skinned alive," though Oriana isn't certain of the legitimacy of that fear. Ms. Black and Dr. Black do not seem terribly violent. Perhaps it is a turn of phrase. The use of her name is also puzzling. Andy has never used it before. She can't really remember the last time someone used her name so casually.

"You said my name," says Oriana.

"Yeah. Should I call you something else? Is there a nickname I should use?"

"Nickname?"

"It's a name friends use. Like, if I started calling you Ana."

"We are friends?"

"I don't know. It's late. I'm exhausted. Just make yourself comfortable and we'll get you back to the house in the morning."

That is not an explanation, but Oriana knows it's the only explanation she's going to get. She begins to stretch out her legs. She shifts her weight, but her wing is throbbing with pain.

"You need help?"

Oriana's face feels hot. She does need help. "My wing…" She instantly regrets it. She should not ask for help. She shouldn't have tried to move. She should stay where she is and figure out a more comfortable position once Andy is asleep.

"The broken one?" asks Andy.

Oriana nods.

"What do you need me to do?"

Oriana doesn't answer. She doesn't *need* anything. Need is weakness. Then again, Oriana *is* weak so perhaps she does need. She's fallen too far, become too comfortable in this strange place. Her shield is completely dissolved. She fears pain to the point that she would do almost anything to avoid it.

For a moment, she's relieved her father is dead. He sacrificed himself so Oriana could be safe and strong. He would not be able to stomach what Oriana has become.

"Does it hurt to move it?" asks Andy. "You probably shouldn't move it on your own."

Her voice pulls Oriana from her thoughts.

"God only knows what you did to it trying to…" Andy stops. "What *were* you trying to do?"

Oriana bites her lip and exhales. "I was trying to fly."

"With one wing?" asks Andy.

"I've flown with a broken wing before."

That's a lie. Oriana's had her wing broken before, but her owner never allowed her the freedom to fly. Other than her ill-fated escape last week, it has been decades since her last flight. Her wings were always bound. She has no idea what compelled her to lie.

"It's still bound. What the hell was your plan?"

Oriana glares. "I was testing the mobility of my uninjured wing," she snaps. She didn't have a plan. She's not ready to admit that. "I was going to unbind the other and—"

"You were escaping."

"Yes." She can't lie about that. It's obvious she was trying to leave. "I realized after speaking with you today that you will not be able to follow through with our deal. I wanted to live my last days my way."

"I'll follow through."

Again, Oriana stops herself from rolling her eyes. "Your bond with your sister won't allow it. My health means a great deal to her. She means a great deal to you, ergo my health means a great deal to you, ergo you will not be able to kill me. This is most likely the reason you're allowing me to stay in your cabin."

Oriana does not know why it took her saying the words out loud for her to understand. Obviously, that's the reason Andy is keeping her here. She is mirroring her sister's kindness.

Andy crosses her arms and for a second Oriana thinks Andy is going to protest the assessment. Instead, she sighs. "Yeah."

"It's all right. Once I realized you and Dr. Black were sisters, I suspected this would be a problem. I understand humans have very strong familial bonds."

Her owner had a family once. Occasionally, during quiet moments brought on with the aid of alcohol, her owner would sit in the silo and talk about his family. He would wait for Oriana to respond or do something he would interpret as an offense, then expel his rage against her. It seemed to comfort him, and in a bizarre way, that comforted Oriana. It was easier to take the pain knowing she deserved it.

Sometimes, after he'd exhausted himself, he would sit beside Oriana and cry silently. After those moments, he would not return to the silo for several days. In that time Oriana would heal, but starve. She'd feel a twisted sort of joy when he would finally come back.

"And angels don't?"

Andy's question pulls Oriana from her thoughts. What were they talking about? "I don't know. I…" She has no idea what triggered that train of thought.

"Sorry," says Andy.

"Do you even know what you are apologizing for?"

"Uh…"

Oriana can't help the smile that tugs at her lips. "You are very different from other humans."

Andy looks away. Oriana isn't sure what happened, but she took a misstep somewhere. "I've made you uncomfortable again."

"No."

"Yes, but I don't know why you insist on denying it."

Andy seems determined to mask her unease. Her denial is almost reflexive. Oriana can't help but wonder what made Andy that way.

Andy rubs a hand over her face. "Okay, yes, I'm uncomfortable. But only because this is new to me and I'm trying not to fuck up."

She frowns, then realizes Andy's anxiety must again be connected to her family. "Or Ava will skin you alive," says Oriana, remembering Andy's earlier comment.

Andy laughs, which confirms that the phrase is not meant to be taken seriously. "Right. Ava and Faith both."

Oriana decides to ask for confirmation just to be sure. "Presumably that is meant metaphorically and not literally?"

"Yeah."

"What does it mean? What is the literal interpretation?"

Andy suddenly goes pale. "Seriously?" She seems to struggle with herself for a moment. When she answers, her voice is gentle. "It just means they'd be mad at me."

"And as a result of their anger?" Why the explanation of the phrase bothers Andy is beyond Oriana.

"They maybe wouldn't talk to me for a while. I guess it would depend on what I did." Andy keeps glancing from the floor to Oriana.

"I think I understand. You are concerned they would be angry, then withhold affection." She wonders if that definition is true for only Andy, or if it applies to all humans. At least she now knows the threat of being "skinned alive" is a metaphor for something unpleasant, but not necessarily bodily harm.

"Listen, I..." Andy's voice trails off. She's obviously uncomfortable.

Oriana has no idea what she's done to trigger this reaction. She grits her teeth as she pushes herself from the bed. "I should go." Standing was a mistake. Pain blossoms from the fractured bones in her wing and spreads like wildfire through her body.

Suddenly, she feels arms wrap around her. Oriana is too tired to pull away. A voice whispers to her, calm and steady.

"Easy, Ana."

Oriana has one hand over her eyes, trying to steady herself. She's dizzy. She feels something nudge her other hand and she realizes she's gripping Andy's shirt.

"Hang on to me for a sec."

She releases the shirt and moves her arm around Andy's neck. Andy leads her over to the couch.

"Can you hang on right here?"

Oriana nods and leans against the couch, freeing Andy of her weight.

Andy goes to the bed and begins to disassemble it. She tugs the mattress onto the floor and drags it over to Oriana. Then she returns to her side and wraps an arm around Oriana's waist.

"Lay on your side with the broken wing up." She lowers Oriana to the floor, supporting the bulk of her weight.

Once she is on her side, Andy crouches next to her. "What hurts?"

"It's just my wing." A wing should not hurt so much. Broken bones were never so debilitating in the past. "But I'm better now. I should go."

"No." Andy's tone is suddenly different. "You're staying here tonight. I'll make sure Ava looks at you in the morning, but you don't need to move anymore. You're going to hurt yourself."

Andy's demeanor has mysteriously changed yet again. At least she does not seem upset anymore.

"Did Faith give you anything for pain?"

"Yes, but I don't know what it's called."

"Is it human medicine? Can you take human medicine?"

Her sudden concern matches that of the doctor. The change is so abrupt and strange that Oriana can't help but laugh. The fact that Andy is a trapper attempting to heal something she would normally kill just adds to the absurdity of it all.

Andy raises an eyebrow. "You want to let me in on the joke?"

"You are treating my injuries." She's fully aware that in her current position, grinning up at Andy from the mattress, she must seem like a lunatic. "This place is full of contradictions."

"Is this like, an angel humor thing?"

It's too much to explain. Oriana is suddenly exhausted. "Never mind."

Andy leaves and soon Oriana hears water running. Andy returns a moment later with a handful of pills, a glass of water, and a newly dampened cloth. "Take this and drink."

For a second, all Oriana can focus on are the little pills in the palm of Andy's hand. She takes a breath, remembers where she is, then props herself up and accepts what she hopes is medicine.

Andy does not release the glass when Oriana reaches for it and drinks. Oriana assumes she must look as tired as she feels. When she finishes, Andy sets the glass on the floor.

"Can I see if your head is hot?"

Oriana nods, only half-listening. She debates asking for more water.

"I'm going to touch your face," says Andy.

Oriana turns her focus from the glass. Andy seems very serious. Perhaps she knows this is going to hurt. Perhaps this is the punishment. Perhaps Oriana was wrong, and Andy is not attempting to heal. It doesn't matter now, because Oriana does not have the energy to get away. She's more vulnerable on the floor. Andy probably knows that.

"I understand," says Oriana, though she doesn't really. She closes her eyes and waits.

She doesn't flinch when a calloused palm touches her forehead. She can't help the little swell of pride in her chest. She exhales deeply. Andy's hand lingers on her forehead. There is no pain.

Oriana sighs. Andy's hand moves, and she can't help but flinch at the change of position. Andy pulls her hand back before Oriana can explain. Andy mutters something, heart pounding loudly again. She covers Oriana with a sheet and sets a pile of blankets nearby. She quickly turns off the overhead light, then settles in on the couch.

Oriana hears the click of the lamp, and the cabin is dark.

"Good night, Oriana," Andy says quietly.

Whatever was happening before, it's clearly over now. Oriana sighs. "Good night, Andy."

CHAPTER FIVE

Oriana seems better in the morning. Ava looks over her and inspects her wings and gives her approval. Andy calls Faith anyway. After she does her inspection with Faith's guidance, Andy relaxes. She can hear Faith smother a laugh through the phone.

"What's so funny?" she asks.

"I'm just picturing you babysitting an angel, especially Oriana. You're both so stubborn. Throw Ava into the mix...I'm surprised things are going so well."

"You've only been gone a day. I think we can handle each other for a while."

"How about a week? We're going to try to wrap up things here and head back over the weekend."

"Yeah, Doc, we can behave for a week."

"You should stay at the house or let Oriana stay in the cabin."

"That was a one-time thing."

"Then stay in the house."

"Why?"

"The house is bigger and it's easier for Oriana to wander off. I'll sleep better if I know there are two sets of eyes watching her in the house *or* if she's in a smaller space where she can't hide."

"Right. Because that's not going to make her feel like a prisoner."

"I know." She sighs. "This is a tough situation. I feel like Oriana has a death wish and I don't know how to treat that."

Faith sounds exhausted. "She's not dying on my watch," says Andy.

"Thanks. I know this goes against your nature, but I really appreciate your help. It's nice to have you on the team." Faith's voice is small and quiet on the other line.

Andy can't help but feel like she betrayed her baby sister all those years ago. "Well, the joke's on me. Turns out I kind of like helping her."

"Just be gentle around her. Tristan talked to her, and she won't say much, but she's seen some shit."

"Like what? Anything I should know about?"

"Hang on." Faith lowers her voice and Andy can hear her shuffling around. "Sorry. I had to make sure Tristan couldn't hear. He's big on patient confidentiality. I am too, but we don't have a guidebook for a case like this. Tristan didn't tell me what they talked about even though I'm her doctor."

"So, we're all flying blind except for Tristan?"

"I hid a recorder in Oriana's room and got most of their conversations from last week." Faith pauses and takes a heavy breath. "I'm going to trust you, Andy. I think you and Ava should know what's going on since Tristan and I aren't there."

Andy laughs. "Sneaking around behind your man's back?"

"This is serious. I'm emailing the files to you. Listen to them but don't take notes. Tristan will snoop when we get back up there. He already knows I don't like that he's keeping this case secret."

"Have you listened to the recordings?"

"Not yet. I haven't been able to get away from him. I might not get a chance to hear them. If there's anything on there I need to know, don't text me. Call."

"Got it. Don't leave a paper trail for the mister."

"Yeah, and don't forward the email to Ava. She's got a bad habit of leaving her computer open. Just play them for her or tell her the info."

"Play them from my laptop?" She could use her phone, but she'd rather have her computer back.

"Yeah."

"You mean the laptop you hid?"

"Oh—shit—yeah, that laptop. I'll tell Ava to give it back."

"You could just tell me where it is."

Faith snorts. "I'm not going to give up my hiding place."

Andy grins. Faith probably hid all her stuff in one place instead of scattering it. Amateur. "All right. I'll wait for your email."

"Thanks. Talk to you later."

"Later."

Ava delivers Andy's laptop, and they agree to listen to the recordings in shifts so one of them can keep an ear out for Oriana.

"You can have the first go," says Ava. "I'm going to take the kid out back and let her get some fresh air. Maybe that'll make her feel better."

"Good luck with that."

"Before I forget, are you moving up to the house, or do you want me to set you and Oriana up in a bigger cabin?"

Andy can feel her face burning. "I—uh—what?"

"Faith wants her under close supervision. I've got cases to manage and people to distract. I could take time off to babysit, but since you're here you might as well pull your weight." Ava crosses her arms, daring Andy to argue.

"Oh." Andy tries to relax. Guilt. It's guilt that keeps tripping her up and making her fumble. She's betraying her father, failing him again. "I'll come up to the house."

"Good. You can take the room next to Oriana. I put some of your stuff up there already. You've got all your necessities, but you're not getting your knives, guns, or acid back."

"Not ever?" whines Andy. Logically, she knows Ava can't stop her from tearing the place apart trying to retrieve her things. But Ava knows all she has to do is put her foot down and Andy will obey.

"Not until I see you have a conversation with that angel without throwing a hissy fit."

"She stayed with me all night last night and I didn't throw a hissy fit!"

"Doesn't count until I see it." She tosses Andy a pair of earbuds and turns on her heels to fetch Oriana from her room upstairs.

Andy huffs, indignant. She's the donkey and her weapons are the carrot. Ava and Faith both know it. Andy goes back to her cabin, packs her few belongings, and prepares to listen to the recordings in seclusion. The fact that she's not bothered by the massive breach of confidentiality should be a red flag, but Andy knows her moral compass is skewed. She's a little surprised that Faith's first instinct is to sneak around and leak private information.

She locks the cabin door. She doesn't know why. No one is going to bother her. She sets up on the couch, pops in the earbuds and hits play. It's just white noise until she hears Tristan's voice.

"May I come in?"

Oriana grunts.

The door creaks, then clicks shut.

"Thank you. I'm Doctor Tristan Naser. You can call me Tristan, if you'd like. I'm a psychiatrist. I'm here to find out how we can make sure you are comfortable while you are with us."

"I am comfortable," says Oriana.

A pause.

"May I sit?"

"You do not need to ask my permission. This is not my home."

"This is your space. As far as we are concerned, nothing can happen in this room without your permission."

"So, if I were to break that window and leap out, you could not stop me without my permission."

Another pause. Longer this time.

"I would not stop you if that's what you really wanted to do."

Oriana snorts. "Liar."

"I know you were a prisoner before. I know you don't expect to be treated fairly. I know you don't want to be here, but please understand, we're not trying to cause you more pain. We just want to help."

Oriana doesn't respond.

"If we let you leave, the person who kidnapped you could find you again. You're injured. You might not be able to get away. And if a trapper finds you, they will kill you. Please understand."

"I am not an animal," growls Oriana. "I understand you are making decisions 'for my own good' despite my wishes."

Tristan sighs. "How about we just talk?"

"We've talked enough."

After another minute or two of silence, Andy hears Tristan get up and leave. She listens until she hears Faith come in to check on Oriana. The angel doesn't say anything. Faith says her wounds are healing as she expected. The recording ends. There are seven recordings total. Session five is longer than the others. Andy skips to it.

Someone knocks on the door.

"Come in," calls Oriana.

"Do you have time to talk?" asks Tristan.

The door shuffles open then clicks shut.

Oriana huffs.

"You can ask me to leave," says Tristan.

"You will come back later."

"You don't want me to come back?"

"It doesn't matter."

A pause.

"If I answer your questions, will you stop coming back?"

"Yes, if that's what you want."

"All right. Then I will answer your questions."

"I want to know your history. You can start wherever you feel comfortable."

"You want to know the worst of what's happened to me so you can find out how damaged I am."

"*I want to know whatever you will tell me. You can tell me only the good memories, if that makes you more comfortable.*"

Someone sighs.

"*Giving birth to me killed my mother. She was human.*"

Another pause.

"*I never knew her. My father was an angel. His wings are mounted above my owner's bed. My owner is a human. Presumably he was away when your wife and her aunt found me.*"

Oriana pauses again. The room is silent.

"*I believe he was keeping me to breed with—with something else. He—I suspect...*" *Oriana's voice shakes slightly as she says,* "*I suspect, if he was gone long enough for Dr. Black and Ms. Black to find me, that he was out trapping. It's possible he's captured someone else. I would like to—I need...*" *Her voice breaks and the room is quiet again.*

Finally, Tristan speaks. "*May I sit beside you?*"

There is a shuffling noise followed by footsteps. The room is quiet for several minutes.

"*He will hurt them,*" *Oriana says quietly.*

"*Who will he hurt?*"

"*I don't know.*"

"*Is that why you tried to escape? You want to go back...to see if he's captured someone else?*"

Oriana doesn't answer.

"*You want to save them?*"

"*I am the only one of my kind, or at least, the only one known to my owner. Without me, he cannot force another angel to breed.*"

"*You know that's not true. If this is his plan, your absence won't stop him. He'll find another way.*"

"*I don't understand why you care. I believe you care. I just don't understand why. I don't understand this place.*"

"*We believe you are equal to us. You are not an object here.*"

"*I'd like to stop talking now,*" *says Oriana. The bite is gone from her voice.*

Silence, followed by footsteps, followed by the door closing. It's ten minutes before Faith comes in to retrieve the recorder. She doesn't speak to Oriana.

Andy hurries to play the next sessions.

True to his word, Tristan doesn't make Oriana talk. Andy doesn't know what he did instead. Faith obviously thought he was talking to Oriana. The last two recordings are more white noise. She plays the other sessions she skipped, but they all go about the same as the first. The only real information is in session five.

Her skin itches. Oriana didn't want to talk, and she probably didn't want anyone other than Tristan to listen. Faith and Andy are the only people with a copy of the sessions, and Faith is going to delete her copy. Andy's finger hovers over the delete button. She'll make an excuse later. She'll say it was an accident. Ava won't be mad, just annoyed. She deletes the files.

Andy shuts her computer, finishes collecting her things, and heads up to the house. When she doesn't find anyone inside, she goes to the backyard.

"You want to take over?" asks Ava. She's leaning against the fence that surrounds what used to be a pasture.

Oriana is standing about fifteen yards away, good wing outstretched with the wind blowing through her feathers.

"You got somewhere to be?" asks Andy.

"Phone's been ringing off the hook all day. I can't talk *and* watch her, *and* look shit up at the same time."

"What exactly do you do all day?"

Ava has a reputation in the trapping world. She's a human search engine for all things magic. But clearly Ava doesn't trap, and Faith wouldn't let her help other trappers.

"I keep people like you from killing people like her," says Ava, pointing to Oriana.

Andy crosses her arms. "And nobody's figured out you've gone rogue?"

"You going to watch her or not?"

So much for that conversation. "I'll watch her." She glances to Oriana, then lowers her voice. "About that email from Faith— the one with Tristan's sessions—I fucked up."

Ava raises an eyebrow.

"I meant to save it, but I deleted it instead."

"Just give me the highlights later."

Andy nods. "Will do." A thought crosses her mind—a bit of information that has been conspicuously absent since she arrived. "Hey, what's the name of the guy who was holding Oriana?" She's praying she doesn't recognize the name.

"We don't have a name. He kept a ton of records on Oriana but no personal information and believe me, we tore the place apart looking."

"Did you get a description from Oriana?"

"We did."

"Any distinguishing features?"

Ava scowls and turns, putting her full focus on Andy. She sighs. "You know I love you, and Faith loves you, and Tristan loves you. We're all happy you're coming around and we're happy to have you back."

"But?"

"But I know we're working against a lifetime of training and it's not going to be undone in a week."

"You don't trust me."

"I trust you eighty percent, but twenty percent of me is worried that if I tell you the little bit we do know about that trapper, you'll track him down and tell him where he can find his angel."

"I wouldn't do that." She hopes it's the truth.

"That's what Faith said. But I'd rather be safe than sorry. I know the truth hurts, but I figure you have a right to know why I'm keeping you in the dark."

Andy doesn't respond. She turns away and leans against the fence. She doesn't hear Ava walk away but she does hear the back door open and close.

CHAPTER SIX

Oriana stands with her feet squared beneath her shoulders. The sun is warm and the grass tickles her ankles. Ava is somewhere behind her, the distance between them growing greater with every breath.

In the back of her mind she's thinking about waking up in Andy's cabin a few hours earlier and how strange it was. Not scary. She didn't wake up afraid or confused. Still, it was strange.

She listens to the wind in the trees that surround the field. A bird sings somewhere above her. It's easier this time. She drifts away. The world quiets. She stares ahead but does not see the mountains obscuring the horizon. She can't tell if the clouds are moving. She's far away, safe. She's in control again. The fact that she can still reach this mental calm is reassuring, but she hates that it's taken her so long to get back to her safe space.

Time passes. She knows because the sun is in a different position than when her trance began. Oriana isn't sure what brought her back to reality. Something changed. There is a new smell in the air, a different heartbeat behind her.

Oriana turns and is startled when she sees Andy instead of Ava.

"Ava had work to do. You can keep doing whatever it is you're doing. I'm just here to make sure you don't take off."

How long has she been standing there? Before she can voice the question, Andy approaches. She's watching Oriana. "I'd leave you alone, but I…"

"You are not allowed to leave me alone. Ms. Black—Ava—said you have one damn job around here and you're going to do it, or so help her."

Ava made two things very clear this morning. One, Oriana should not address her as Ms. Black because no one else does and it is weird when Oriana does it. She also said to call Dr. Black "Faith," because that's her name.

She'd said, "You call Andy, Andy, don't you?"

That turned out to be a rhetorical question. Two, Andy is on her best behavior and Ava will make sure she stays that way, though Oriana still isn't entirely sure what that means.

Andy laughs. "That sounds like her."

"It should sound like her. It was a direct quote." She wonders if she misspoke.

Andy laughs again. It's a strangely comforting sound. "It's an expression. Never mind. Point is, I've got to keep an eye on you."

"Your expressions are confusing."

"I know. I'm sorry. I'll try to keep the expressions to a minimum."

Andy seems sincerely sorry for the confusion. Something like guilt passes over her face.

Oriana wonders if Andy lives constantly on the edge of an apology. She can't remember how many times she apologized last night, but it was certainly more than what was necessary. Andy really should never apologize to Oriana. In terms of class and rank, Andy is above her. Andy can say whatever she wants.

Oriana feels her wings twitch like she's a child who hasn't learned to control them. She decides to change her train of thought. "Thank you for sharing your residence with me last night."

Andy shifts her focus to the ground. "Welcome," she mutters.

"Ava said it was—I am paraphrasing—she said it was rare for you to share anything with anyone other than Dr. Black... Faith."

Andy does not look up from the ground. Oriana feels a bizarre desire to regain her attention.

"Ava also said—again, I am paraphrasing—"

"You don't have to always say when you're paraphrasing."

Oriana takes a moment to revel in her success. She's careful not to let her wings reflect her joy. "She said you are going to stay in the house now."

"I am. Moved my stuff into the room beside you. Ava's orders."

Ava does give Andy orders. Oriana has witnessed it. She also gives Faith and Tristan orders. They respect her as one would respect a commander, but they do not always behave like her subordinates. Oriana can't help herself. Curiosity gets the better of her and she must ask. "Ava is not your owner, nor is she your mother. And yet you obey her."

Andy frowns. "She's...I guess—yeah, it's weird."

Oriana accepts that as the only explanation she is going to get. She wonders if she should mirror Andy's behavior around Ava.

"Another issue," she begins. "You called me 'Ana' last night. This is a sign of friendship, correct? The others are not my friends?"

"No, they're your friends. Nicknames usually mean friendship, but not all friends give each other nicknames."

So, nicknames are not an absolute. Ava may never refer to her as "Ana."

"Should I give you a nickname?"

"Andy is a nickname. It's short for Andrea."

"Ah. What are the criteria for a nickname?"

Andy sighs and Oriana almost tells her to forget the question.

"There aren't any criteria," says Andy.

Oriana frowns because how can one establish a nickname if there are no criteria?

Andy answers like she can read Oriana's mind. "It's complicated. Sometimes it's just a shortened version of a name or sometimes it's based on the way somebody acts. There are a lot of—um—variables, I guess."

"Do all humans do this, or is it limited to the humans in your family?"

"I don't know about *all* humans, but *a lot* of humans use nicknames. It's not just us."

Just as Oriana begins to form her next question about the names of Andy's family members, Andy says, "We do use nicknames, though. Just not all the time." She scratches the back of her head. "I'm not a great example of typical human behavior."

"Your behavior is fascinating, though. What do you do that is not 'typical human behavior'?"

Andy sighs and sits in the grass. She motions for Oriana to do the same, so she does.

Andy begins explaining "manners" and how she has none but Faith does. Oriana cannot help but inquire further. She keeps Andy talking until the sun begins to set. She voices less than half her questions, but Andy answers all of them, nonetheless.

During dinner, Ava and Andy discuss their pasts. Andy is insistent that Ava should disclose her "trade secrets," but Ava shares nothing. Instead, she dismisses Andy's questions, and gets up to refill her drink, taking Oriana's glass with her.

"I don't get how everyone knows what Faith does, but no one knows what you do," says Andy.

"I don't answer stupid questions. Just like I'm doing with you right now."

Andy rolls her eyes.

Ava returns to the table and hands Oriana her glass rather than setting it down. When Oriana reaches for it, she realizes why. There is a small note attached to the side of it, concealed first by Ava's hand and now her own.

Oriana waits until Andy isn't looking, then takes the note and unfolds it in her lap below the table. It's written in Ava's scrawling handwriting.

When you're finished eating, go to Andy's cabin and bring back all the alcohol you can find. I'll keep Andy busy. She's probably got a few hiding places in the cabin. Turn the hallway light off, then back on when you're done. I can see it from where I'm sitting. Take whatever you find back to your room. I'll get it from you later.

Oriana frowns at the note and looks up at Ava, but she is deliberately not meeting her gaze. If her accounts of Andy's drinking are any indication, then Andy drinks alcohol like Oriana disassociates.

Oriana sighs, just loud enough for Ava to understand that this is not something she wants to do, then excuses herself from the table. She leaves them arguing over past cases and goes outside instead of to her room.

This is a thinly veiled test of her trust. Ava trusts Oriana not to attempt another escape. If Oriana wants to continue to enjoy the freedoms she has here, she will comply. She does not want to be locked in the recovery room like she was during her first week here.

She huffs, though no one is around to react to her displeasure. She decides to distract herself by turning her mission into an exercise in speed. She was very fast when she was younger. She wonders if her body remembers.

Twenty minutes later, she's back in the house standing at the top of the stairs, panting. She used to be much faster. She has several bottles of alcohol in her arms. She flicks the light switch with her free hand. She leaves the bottles in the corner of her room by the door. She covers them with a towel in the event Andy enters the room on her way to bed.

Several minutes later, she hears the door to the neighboring room click shut. She sits on the edge of her bed and waits.

An hour later, Oriana hears Ava go to Andy's room first, presumably to make sure she is asleep. She enters Oriana's room and takes a sharp inhale, startled.

"I thought you'd be asleep," whispers Ava.

"I was waiting for you."

Ava glances at the towel in the corner. "That it?"

"Yes, you were correct. She was hiding alcohol."

"Where?"

Oriana frowns. Technically, she isn't betraying Andy by telling Ava her secrets. She has no loyalty to Andy. It shouldn't bother her that Ava is using her to violate Andy's privacy. "In a small cabinet above the sink."

She's never been a good liar. There was no alcohol in the cabin. Andy hid her stash in a bag beneath the front porch. It was easy for Oriana to find because she could smell it.

Ava does not look convinced, but she doesn't push Oriana to say more. "Since you're up, I could use some help clearing out the rest of the house."

"Clearing the house?"

Ava nods, then stoops to collect Oriana's bottles. "Yeah. I want this whole place bone dry when she wakes up."

"You shouldn't do that." Oriana cannot stop herself.

"I know. It's really going to piss her off. But I'm not going to be around forever and I'd like to see her healthy before I kick the bucket."

"In what way does Andy's health relate to you assaulting a bucket?"

"It's a saying. Means before I die."

Ava does not wait for Oriana to respond. She walks out of the room, leaving the door open behind her. Oriana recognizes that as an order masked as an invitation. She sighs again and follows Ava downstairs.

There is already a collection of bottles and cans on the kitchen table. Ava pulls a small metal container from her pocket and adds it to the assortment. It's Andy's. Oriana has seen her drinking from it. Ava must have stolen it from Andy's room.

"We'll start in the kitchen. Shouldn't take too long."

"What will you do to me if I refuse to assist?"

"I'll tell you to go back to bed and I'll ask you to let me be the one to tell Andy her booze is gone." She is currently rummaging through a cabinet beside the refrigerator. She pulls out a bag.

"I mean in terms of punishment," says Oriana. She wonders if it's worse to know in advance or to be surprised.

"Nobody gets punished here. I told you that already."

"Then what is my motivation for obeying you?"

Ava sighs and stops what she's doing. "You don't have to obey me. You *never* have to obey me. You should only do what you want to do."

That can't be entirely true. Oriana wants to leave but she can't. She isn't being forced to help, but Ava clearly wants her to. What would she do instead of helping Ava? If she were not helping in the quest to rid the house of liquor and beer, she'd be upstairs dreading the next round of nightmares. At least this way she is useful.

She owes these people that much, doesn't she? Their kindness should be rewarded. They probably expect it. She doesn't respond to Ava. Instead, she goes to the refrigerator and begins pulling out cans of beer.

It's well into the night when they finish. Ava pours out all the beer. She takes the liquor and Andy's flask and locks them away in the large safe in her room. Oriana stands in the doorway and watches her open the safe, taking care to pay attention to the combination. She catches a glimpse of some of Andy's other belongings.

Andy must know what it's like to be trapped. This is most likely the reason she agreed to end Oriana's life. Does Andy have an escape plan? She dismisses the thought. Andy is human. She has more rights than Oriana. Someone would free her if it was what she really wanted.

Ava bids her a curt good night and thanks her for the help. Oriana goes back to her room repeating the combination to the safe in her head. The numbers are firmly ingrained in her memory as she pulls her mattress onto the floor.

She crawls carefully to the center of the mattress and lays on her side. The sheet is soft and warm. She didn't realize how nice it was to prop her head on a pillow until Andy made her sleep that way. She pulls the blanket over her and up to her chin. It's nice, cozy, safe. She closes her eyes and tries to make her muscles soft like the mattress is soft. Her limbs are heavy. With every exhale, her body sinks a little deeper into the bed.

She does not remember going back. She does not remember leaving Ava's home. But when she wakes up, she is on the rough dirt floor of her cage instead of the soft mattress in her room.

She stands and tries to take a step, but finds her foot is shackled to the floor. Both wings are bound with hard leather and pressed tightly against her back.

A familiar laugh echoes through the silo. Maybe he'll tell Oriana what he wants this time. Maybe there will be a right answer.

Oriana can't see him yet, but she can hear metal on metal. What tool is that? She can't remember, but she knows the pain that follows it.

She tries to call for Ava, but her voice catches, and she can't make the words come out.

Suddenly, her owner is behind her. Oriana lets out a shriek as he snaps one of her primary feathers in half, then rips it from her wing.

Oriana is on her knees. He is speaking, but Oriana can't hear him. She tries to scream again. She's exhausted. She's not as strong as she was at Ava's. She doesn't know when the weakness came creeping back. It's familiar, suffocating.

She didn't deserve all that strength anyway. She hasn't earned the right to be strong. What would she do with it? She'd hurt someone. That's what monsters do, they hurt. And Oriana is a monster.

Someone calls her name.

He snaps another feather, and the pain is blinding. She freezes. This is punishment.

Sometimes, her owner demands that she fight back. Her owner wants to be stronger when he goes out trapping. Oriana is not a good opponent. She is too slow, too reluctant, too tired, too sick.

Something hits her and she's pressed face-first into the dirt. He pins Oriana to the ground and shouts for her to be still.

Oriana obeys. She always obeys. She fears pain. She'll do anything to avoid it. She tries to prepare herself. She breathes.

The smell is wrong.

The cage smells sweet and warm. The person behind her smells like soap instead of blood and sweat. Someone calls her Ana.

Oriana's eyes snap open and she gasps. She is pinned down, but she's on a mattress. Someone is on top of her.

Suddenly, the weight of the other person is gone. They back away from the mattress and Oriana can see her in the moonlight. It's the trapper. She has a name, but Oriana can't remember it. She backs away from the mattress until she meets the wall. She slides down to the floor, panting and pale. She doesn't look injured. She looks upset. Slowly, she braces a shaking hand against the wall. She gets to her feet and approaches Oriana with caution.

Oriana closes her eyes. She hears slow footsteps on the carpet. Familiar fingers brush against the back of her hand.

"I'm sorry," she whispers.

Oriana waits, unsure of the woman at the edge of the mattress.

She gently holds Oriana's hand. "Ana?" she asks. "You with me?"

Oriana frowns. That seems familiar too. She opens her eyes.

"I fucked up," she says. "I shouldn't have pinned you like that."

Andy. The woman kneeling beside her is Andy.

"I forgot what I was doing for a second. I just wanted you to stop. I thought you might hurt yourself." Andy's voice wavers. "I wasn't going to hurt you."

She's dizzy and her skin is too warm. She pulls her hand away from Andy and lays her head against her arms. Maybe she will wake up soon.

She hears Andy leave. She hears shuffling in the other room. She hears footsteps moving away from her. She sits up and checks her wings. The broken one is bound, but the other is free. She's still at Ava's.

Andy is sorry again.

She said she "pinned" Oriana. Andy clearly thought it was a bad thing to do. It wasn't pleasant but it didn't hurt. Something about that upset Andy. Maybe it was instinct. Maybe humans react automatically in certain situations. Andy's pulse was certainly high enough for her to be prepared for fight or flight.

She hears the humans speaking. Then someone comes back upstairs. The door to her room opens.

"You okay?" asks Ava, switching on the light.

Oriana nods.

"Downstairs. Follow me."

"What happened?"

Ava doesn't answer. She turns and leaves the door open again. Oriana sighs and follows her. Andy is sitting in a chair in the middle of the kitchen, a distant expression on her face. Ava pulls a stool next to Andy's chair and gestures to Oriana. Once they are both seated, Ava faces them.

"Now, what happened? Somebody explain." She crosses her arms and waits.

Andy answers quickly, almost automatically. "It's my fault. Oriana was having a nightmare. She was kind of flailing. I wanted her to stop. I got her in a kill position and she woke up." Andy's voice is quiet, repentant.

"Okay. Version one. Oriana, what's version two?"

Oriana does not know how to answer. Andy's version was accurate. "I had a nightmare," she begins. "I cannot speak to my behavior while I was unconscious, but I am sure I was violent. I usually am. I awoke and Andy was restraining me." She leaves out the part where she momentarily forgot that Andy was not her owner.

"Is anybody hurt?"

Andy answers "no" at the same moment as Oriana.

"Are you two mad at anybody besides me?"

"No," answers Oriana.

Andy says nothing. She could be mad.

Oriana would not begrudge her anger. After all she's done to prove she isn't like other trappers, Oriana forgot her in a moment of panic. She frowns. She is indebted to these people, to Andy. She owes them.

Their kindness isn't free. Kindness is never free. Something like acid sticks in the back of her throat. She is tired of being beholden to humanity. She is tired of paying a price for things she did not ask to receive.

"Andy?" asks Ava. "You mad?"

"No, but, Ana, I thought—"

"I am ashamed of my behavior." That is the appropriate thing to say, isn't it? Isn't that what she should feel, shame? "I dislocated your sister's shoulder during a similar fit. You were right to restrain me. I could have hurt you."

"But I thought—you wouldn't talk. I thought you were mad."

"I was not myself in that moment. Forgive me." She's angry, but she doesn't understand why. She wants to leave. She suddenly finds herself longing for the solitude of her cage.

"All right," says Ava. "Ground rules. Rule One, Andy, hands to yourself. Don't touch Oriana without her permission; I don't care how much you think you're helping."

That's an odd rule, odd enough that it brings Oriana's attention back to the present. Ava lists a series of rules that are presumably meant to make their lives easier, but they seem awkward and cumbersome to remember.

"Per Rule Two," she says, once Ava is done talking, "I wish to report this conversation as something I don't like."

For some reason, Andy laughs.

"Noted," says Ava. "I don't think anybody likes this. You still have to sit through it."

That does not seem fair. Then again, Ava is the one who made the rules; she can break them.

Ava is watching Andy. "Why'd you try to run?"

Oriana can sense Andy's heart rate increase.

"If we're going to do this, I need a drink," Andy says.

Oriana flinches.

"Good luck," says Ava. "I got rid of all the booze after you went to bed."

Andy goes pale. "All of it?"

"All of it. You're going to do this sober. Why'd you try to run?"

Oriana feels a sudden urge to explain to Andy that she can meditate instead of drinking.

"Oriana had a nightmare, and I went from comfort to kill like that," says Andy, snapping her fingers. Her voice is shaky again. "You, Faith, and Tristan have a good thing going here and I'm not somebody you need hanging around."

Oriana watches Andy. She is not mocking her. She seems to be serious. She is taking responsibility for what happened. After more conversation, Andy falls silent. She isn't looking up. She is obviously uncomfortable. Ava should not make her do this without her coping mechanism.

"You both need to detox," says Ava. "Andy, you need to detox in more ways than one."

Oriana watches for a reaction from Andy, but she only glances up to look at Ava before returning her gaze to the floor. The way she reacts to Ava is strange. They are not commander and warrior as Oriana previously thought. Ava is obviously disrespecting Andy's boundaries, but not in a cruel way, because she is not cruel. She is scolding Andy, the way a mother would scold a child.

"I don't want you to make an exception for Oriana," continues Ava. "Faith and I have wanted you to help us for a long time. We could use your expertise. I'd be lying if I said I wasn't going to try to change you."

"You are making Andy uncomfortable," says Oriana. Maybe Ava does not realize what she's doing.

Andy looks up.

"I'm aware," says Ava.

"I am uncomfortable as well."

"I know," says Ava. She either doesn't understand or doesn't care.

"I don't like it," clarifies Oriana. At this point, she's testing to see if Rule Two will ever be upheld. She needs to know.

This time, Ava seems to understand. "Okay. Enough for tonight. You two going to be all right until the morning?"

"I'll be better once you stop talking," says Andy. She almost smiles and her voice is steady again.

Ava rolls her eyes. "All right, jackass. You're both dismissed."

Andy leaves the kitchen quickly and Oriana follows. She is not as angry as she was before. She's not sure what she's feeling now. Andy stops at the top of the stairs and motions for Oriana to follow her. Curiosity wins over exhaustion and Oriana follows Andy into her bedroom. She replays the last part of their conversation. She has gained privileged insight into Andy's history. She suspects it will be useful later.

"I'm not going to talk forever, like Ava," says Andy, once the door is shut. She mutters something else.

"I believe I understand your relationship with her now," says Oriana slowly. "She fills the position of the mother in your family." Andy doesn't answer so Oriana continues, "She is, of course, not your mother, but since my arrival, I've heard your father mentioned, but never your mother. She is missing. Ava takes her place as the protector and guardian of you and Faith."

"That's...accurate. I've never thought about it before."

Oriana nods, pleased to have figured out their relationship. It makes their group easier to understand, because they are a family, not a squadron.

"I'm sorry for what I did earlier," says Andy. "I know you told Ava you weren't mad—"

"I'm not angry," says Oriana. She wonders how many times Andy will apologize for the same mistake. "I was afraid." Oriana isn't sure if she said it aloud this time. She suddenly realizes she's staring at the floor.

"I know. There are better ways to stop a nightmare. I just—I suck at this."

Oriana did say it aloud. She confessed. She's not sure if that makes it better. "I was not afraid of *you*," she clarifies. "I am stronger than you, even injured. I simply forgot myself for a moment."

She didn't fight back when Andy held her down. For all her newfound strength, all her rage against humanity, she didn't fight back. She gave up and let it happen.

"How often do you have nightmares?"

"Every night, except for last night." She did not dream last night.

"I get nightmares too, but I didn't get them last night either."

Strange that their nights of restful sleep would coincide. She's never felt peace with a human around. Why would she find peace with Andy?

"I will let you sleep," says Oriana. "Good night, Andy."

Andy goes back to her room. She shuts the door and returns to her mattress. She's haunted. She's haunted by the way Oriana looks at her, by Ava and Faith and their hope that she'll change. She's haunted by her father and the truth about his death.

She shivers. Her father wouldn't want her to tell—wouldn't want Faith to know. She tries to force the memory back down, but it keeps bubbling to the surface.

She can still see her mother, graceful and kind, grinning as she holds her arms out to Jeremy. It's not her, not really. She looks exactly like Andy remembers, the monster's energy keeping her body young and alive. Andy hadn't been prepared for that.

Jeremy had told her and Faith that he'd destroyed their mother's body, that the demon found a different body.

Andy's not reacting like she should. She's still in shock. She can't fight this thing. She can't fight her mother. What if she's still in there? What if Faith can bring her back? It's hope that got her father killed.

Andy shakes herself from the memory. She can't afford to dwell on the past.

The next night Oriana does have another nightmare. The first scream wakes Andy, but by the second scream, Ava is already up the stairs and into her room. Andy feels a twinge of shame because Ava must think Andy can't handle this. She doesn't trust Andy not to fuck up again. She hangs back and watches Ava calm the thrashing angel.

She's surprised by Ava's technique. Ava kneels by the mattress. She pulls her phone from her pocket and starts playing gentle music. It takes a few seconds for the sounds to reach Oriana, but eventually she releases her grip on the sheets and stops fighting. She stills, breathing heavily.

Ava stops the song, stands and motions for Andy to follow. She nudges Andy toward her room. "Your mama taught me that trick when I use to babysit you and your sister. Faith showed me how to play music on the phone. My singing voice isn't what it used to be." She chuckles quietly to herself. "Go back to sleep. I'll stay on angel duty for a while."

Andy just nods and returns to her room. She's suddenly exhausted.

CHAPTER SEVEN

In the morning, Ava knocks on Oriana's door and sends her and Andy into the kitchen for breakfast. There are two sheets of paper on the table between their plates.

Andy reaches the table first and groans as she picks up the paper. "Chores? Seriously? Are we twelve?"

Oriana examines the other sheet, unfamiliar with "chores." She peers over Andy's shoulder to see if their papers are the same, which they are.

"I'm putting you to work," says Ava.

"I thought my job was watching her," says Andy, pointing to Oriana.

"You can multitask. Coffee?"

She offers a mug to each of them. Oriana has come to enjoy coffee, though Faith is better at making it.

"Ana isn't ready to do half the shit you have listed," says Andy.

Ava sets a plate with eggs and meat on the table.

"I can do all of these tasks," says Oriana.

"Faith wouldn't want you to," says Andy.

"That's why you're going to help her," says Ava.

Andy mutters something about "free labor."

"I could accomplish these faster on my own," says Oriana.

"Not if you want to heal on time," says Andy.

Oriana doesn't offer a retort, as Andy is watching her with one eyebrow raised.

"You want to share something with the class?" asks Ava.

"No," answers Andy. "Just pointing out the obvious." She spoons eggs onto her plate, then does the same for Oriana. "Say when."

"When," says Oriana.

"No, not like...I mean tell me when you want me to stop putting eggs on your plate."

"Oh, you can stop now—um—when. Stop when?"

"Close enough. Want bacon?"

Oriana nods.

Ava is grinning down at her plate.

They eat breakfast with Andy self-correcting anytime she uses an expression. When they are finished, Ava sends them away from the house.

"Want to knock out—er—work on the hardest stuff first?" asks Andy.

"We don't have to adhere to a certain order?"

Andy leads them through the house and out into the garage. "I doubt it. We're doing Ava a favor so she can take it or leave it."

"This is a favor?" Oriana frowns at the paper in her hand.

"Technically, yeah. We don't *have* to do her stupid chores."

"What would we do instead?"

Andy is rummaging through a box of tools. "I don't know. What do you want to do? And don't say 'die' or 'escape.'"

"Fly."

Andy looks over her shoulder at Oriana. "Fly?"

"Maybe more than I want to leave."

Andy shoves her list of tasks into the pocket of her jeans. She turns and examines Oriana, chewing on her bottom lip.

"You can't fly. Not yet. But I think I know something you might enjoy." She nods to the garage door. "Meet me out back."

Intrigued, Oriana does as she's told. She waits for Andy on the back porch. She hears something like a roar echo across the field as a vehicle pulls around the corner of the house. Andy gets out and motions for Oriana to approach.

"Get in the back," she says. The back of the vehicle is flat and open with short sides around the open back. "Just make sure you hang on."

Oriana clambers onboard and finds something to hold on to. Andy resumes her position behind the steering wheel. She opens a pane of glass behind her that separates the interior of the vehicle from the exterior. "Knock once if you want me to slow down, twice if you want me to speed up. If you want me to stop the truck, just grab my shoulder. I'll leave the window open."

"All right," says Oriana.

She braces herself, but Andy eases the "truck" into a slow start. Oriana knocks twice on the glass. She hears Andy laugh over the sound of rubber on gravel. The truck accelerates. Oriana tentatively spreads her wing. The wind is magnificent, refreshing. She stands and leans over the top of the truck, wing angled forward as if she were flying. She grins, reaches down, and knocks twice on the glass again.

She's not sure how long they stay out. They don't talk. Andy just drives and lets Oriana enjoy the ride. She keeps them on an open dirt road that surrounds Ava's property. The house grows distant but never leaves sight. Oriana waits until they reach the point on the road where they are the farthest away from the house. She retracts her wing, then crouches back down. She knocks once and Andy slows the truck. She taps Andy's shoulder and Andy brings the truck to a stop. She turns around in her seat. "You okay?"

"Yes, I have a question."

"Okay."

"If you know how to operate this truck, why don't you use it to leave? Or do you not want to leave?"

"My stuff's still here."

"You cannot leave without your stuff?"

"I can, but I don't want to."

Oriana hums. "I see."

A crease forms between Andy's eyebrows. "Hey, Ana?"

"Yes?"

"Do you still want to, you know"—she clears her throat—"are we still sticking with the two-week plan?"

Oriana frowns back at her. "I'm not sure." She finds it hard to believe that such a small amount of time could undo a decades-long death wish. "If I do decide to die, I will not require your help."

Andy does not want to kill her. It would be unfair to make her do it.

"I gave you my word. I'll be there if you decide that's what you want to do. I won't make you go out alone."

"It will upset you."

"Quit worrying about me getting upset. I said I'll do it and I meant it."

Oriana tilts her head to the side. She does worry about upsetting Andy, more than she realized.

Andy sighs. "I know where you're coming from." She leans closer to the open window between them and Oriana moves closer so she can hear Andy better.

"I've been there. I've wanted the same thing. Hell, I even tried to off myself once or twice. But shit changes. Life gets different. Things can get better or worse in the blink of an eye."

Oriana clenches her jaw. "How?"

"I don't know, stuff happens."

"No, how did you try to kill yourself?"

"I'll tell you later if you're still around. I'm not going to give you tips."

Oriana scowls. She wasn't asking for advice. Things that would kill a human would not necessarily kill an angel, even a mongrel like Oriana.

"I want you to *want* to live, but if, when this week is over, you still want to die, I'll be the one to do it."

"I can do it alone." She doesn't mean to be dismissive. She wants Andy to know she isn't obligated to help.

"I'm the professional killer. I won't back out of our deal. I promise. Just finish out the week and let me know what you decide."

Oriana looks for a break, a sign of insincerity in Andy's eyes, but finds none. "All right."

The return trip to the house is quiet. Oriana doesn't pretend to fly.

Ava lectures Andy for taking the truck but Andy seems unmoved by her words. After Ava returns to her office, Andy grins and says Ava is "a big teddy bear."

They take the truck out again the next day. Andy does not bring up their agreement. They've yet to accomplish any of the tasks on the list Ava assigned them and tomorrow is theoretically Oriana's last day alive. She feels like she should do something useful.

Andy is making her way to the backyard where the truck is parked and Oriana stops her. "We should address our chores today."

"You don't want to ride?"

"Maybe later, but we should do something useful first."

Andy shrugs. "All right, but don't hurt yourself."

"With the exception of my wing, my injuries are healed."

"That's great, but you still have to take it easy. Doctor's orders."

Oriana tilts her head to the side, eyeing Andy. Faith did not tell Oriana she needed to "take it easy." And if this was an order from the doctor, then Ava would not contradict it by giving them chores. "Does this concern actually come from Faith or does it come from you?"

Andy turns away from her but her demeanor changes. "We'll fix the fence today. Meet me out front." With that, Andy leaves.

Oriana goes to the front yard as instructed. She can hear banging coming from the garage, but she doesn't leave her post. She waits.

Andy finally arrives. She's driving the truck. It is full of supplies. Oriana scowls at her as she parks the truck by the fence. "You gathered supplies on your own." Andy has turned the vehicle off and is now unloading large slats of wood. "That was deliberate."

"What was?"

Oriana moves to help, but Andy blocks her. "You are very stubborn," says Oriana.

"You're still healing."

"We've already addressed this."

Andy blocks her way again. This time she faces Oriana and hands her a small metal object. "If you want to help, you can measure the wood."

Oriana clenches her jaw and takes the device. She fumbles with it before figuring out the correct way to use it. By the time she has completed her assignment, Andy has finished unloading the truck.

Oriana tries not to dwell on her frustration because "stewing" is against Rule Three, but Andy is being deliberately obstinate. She assigns Oriana small, tedious tasks to keep her busy. Oriana cannot decide if she is being punished or coddled. Andy doesn't look angry or annoyed. She actually seems pleased and even has the gall to grin at Oriana when their eyes meet.

Andy finally steps away from the fence, examining her work. Oriana waits for Andy to order her to fetch the hammer or find a different attachment for the drill, or something equally inane.

"Thanks for your help. Looks good."

Oriana bites her tongue. Andy is mocking her. She must be. Oriana made no significant contributions to the job. In an attempt to preserve her last remaining ounce of patience, and maybe a little bit out of spite, Oriana decides to distract herself with conversation. "How did you lose your mother?"

Andy freezes. She stares ahead, unblinking before she answers, "She died."

Andy's reaction is all the encouragement Oriana needs to continue. She feels a twisted sense of victory now that the discomfort has shifted to Andy. "Did you know her?"

"Yes."

"You loved her deeply."

"Yes."

"How did she die?"

Andy shifts her weight, still staring at the fence. "Something killed her."

Oriana suspects she is treading into dangerous territory, but this is no less than Andy deserves. She was beginning to feel like Andy's equal until they started working together. "Something like me?" She assumes as much, but a vindictive part of her wants to make Andy say it. "It's why you kill."

"Yes. We weren't sure at first, but Dad tracked it down."

Oriana is surprised that Andy is still answering her questions. "What became of your father?"

Andy takes a moment to answer. "Something killed him too."

"He died recently, correct?"

This time Andy doesn't answer, she just stares. Oriana moves closer and repeats the question.

Andy still doesn't answer.

Oriana steps between her and the fence. Andy does not look angry. Her eyes are unfocused and her lips are parted. "Andy?"

No response. She is miles away, hypnotized by something Oriana cannot see.

"Andy?"

Oriana has pushed her too far. Instead of vindicated, Oriana is guilty and panicked. She moves closer and grabs Andy by her shoulder, shaking her gently. "Andy, can you hear me? Please respond."

At last, Andy blinks and her eyes seem to focus again.

"Andy?" Oriana cannot stop saying her name. She needs an answer before she can calm down.

She finally seems to see Oriana. "Sorry," she breathes. "I spaced out for a second."

Oriana studies Andy, her panic not yet subsided. "You are unwell," she says slowly. "We should return to the house."

Andy blinks again and her eyes begin to wander. Oriana holds a hand to her face to keep her focused. She should call for Ava. Andy leans into Oriana's touch and seems to relax.

Oriana doesn't dare move her hand. "I should not have tried to pry. I was attempting to…I upset you. It was selfish. I apologize." She can't bring herself to confess. She feels small, childish.

"It's okay," says Andy. She is fully focused on Oriana now. "You lost your mom too. We've got something in common."

Oriana's heart breaks. She is unfit for this world.

"What happened to your dad?"

She owes Andy an answer. "My owner killed him."

Andy takes a slow breath.

Oriana moves her thumb against Andy's cheek. The physical contact seems to help. "This calms you. You did something similar in the cabin." She tries to remember the way Andy touched her face when she thought Oriana was sick. She repositions her hand. "You said you were checking for a fever, but I suspect, though, this type of touch is meant to soothe." She hopes she's right.

Andy has also used humor to defuse a tense situation. A faint smile ghosts across Andy's lips. "Yeah."

Oriana mentally braces herself and makes an attempt at sarcasm. "If I wake you again in the night, this would be a nice alternative to kneeing me in the back."

Andy laughs. "Are you giving me permission?"

Oriana cannot help but laugh too as relief floods through her and replaces guilt. "Yes, in accordance with the rules set down by Ava, you have my permission to do this the next time I have a nightmare."

Andy is staring at her now, still grinning. Her eyes are focused, and the attention is more intense than Oriana anticipated. Heat rises in her body and she drops her hand. She feels dizzy and warm. The sensation is not bad. She hurt Andy, but she was also able to heal her. She has never healed anyone before, never done anything helpful before.

She does not know what Andy is thinking as she continues to stare, but she knows something significant has transpired between them and it cannot be undone.

Andy was right. Life changes in the blink of an eye.

CHAPTER EIGHT

Andy finds Oriana and Ava asleep in the living room the next morning. Ava is out cold in her recliner and Oriana is curled onto her side beneath a blanket on the sofa bed. They each have an empty coffee mug on the floor beside them.

Andy collects their dishes and decides to start breakfast. Faith called her earlier in the morning and woke her. Andy would rather be asleep, but she's too jittery to go back to bed.

Oriana is almost completely healed. It's her angel side kicking in. If she was human, she would have died from the injuries she sustained. Faith said Oriana will probably be able to fly soon, but she doesn't want Oriana to try it while she's not there.

Today is the last day. Oriana might be ready to die. Andy has to be ready too.

She cracks eggs into a bowl and wonders how she's going to keep Oriana grounded until Faith comes back. Flying makes Oriana happy, and if she's happy, maybe she'll want to live. She beats the eggs and pours them into a frying pan, then moves on to the bacon. She hears the couch creak in the living room. She pours two cups of coffee. She doesn't need to turn around to know Oriana has come into the kitchen. Maybe it's because she's been a killer for so long and she knows the signs of an angel approaching. Maybe she just knows Oriana.

"Faith called," says Andy. "She said we might be able to unbind that wing." She grabs Oriana's coffee cup. "She said she doesn't want you to fly until she gets back, but you should be able to move it." She turns and hands Oriana the cup. "She said she wants you to do some physical therapy crap before you fly. I can help if you want."

"Thank you," says Oriana. Her voice is low and sleepy. Their fingers touch as Oriana takes her cup. She frowns at Andy. "Why does your face do that?"

Fuck.

"Do what?" Andy knows what, but she asks anyway.

"Turn colors."

Andy rubs her face. "Because I'm a dumbass."

Oriana does that curious head tilt thing.

"It's a stupid human thing."

"Do I do it?"

Andy chuckles, because yeah, Oriana blushes too and it's fucking adorable. "Sometimes."

"What causes it?"

"Feelings," mutters Andy. She's staring at the floor. That's the best answer she's got. "Sometimes they make you blush and feel like an idiot."

"Blush?"

"The color change." Andy turns back to the stove before she embarrasses herself further. "It's called blushing." She flips the bacon.

Oriana seems to take a moment to let that process. "Andy." She sounds serious when she speaks again. "I need to explain my behavior yesterday."

"Don't worry about it. It was just a weird thing. I get it. I thought it was weird too. I mean it was nice at the time. But now, totally weird." It was *very* nice. Oriana touched her face and Andy felt like melting.

"You thought it was nice?"

Andy whips around to face her. She's a fucking moron. "No, I thought you thought it was nice." She doesn't exactly hear what Oriana says next. Her heart is pounding too loudly. Can Oriana hear it? "Don't worry about it. I hadn't even thought about it until you mentioned it."

"You're not angry or hurt?"

"No." She hopes she sounds casual enough. "Of course not. You were just trying to help. It was my fault anyway. You were just following my lead, but I told you, I'm a shitty role model."

Andy goes back to cooking and Oriana decides to stand right beside her. "I'm not sure we're talking about the same thing."

"What are you talking about?" She tries not to hope this is a misunderstanding.

"The way I questioned you yesterday. I knew it would upset you. I did it on purpose."

Andy lets out a breath she didn't know she was holding. "Oh, Jesus, that's—that's it? That's all you meant?"

"Yes. What did you think I was talking about?"

The nice, soft, weird, but good-weird, way you touched my face.

"I don't know, I guess I just panicked. I don't know what I thought."

If Oriana thinks that's bullshit, she doesn't call her on it. "I need to apologize. I was angry with you and deliberately caused you pain that was unequal to the pain you caused me."

The floor drops out from underneath Andy. Oriana was angry? When was she angry? When did she cause Oriana pain? Fuck. She knew she shouldn't have let her help with that stupid fucking fence.

She looks Oriana over for any sign of injury. "What pain? Why were you angry? What did I do? I'm sorry." She doesn't mean to vomit words, but she does.

"Not physical pain. I was upset. I do not fully understand why, but—"

"When were you upset?"

Oriana was quiet yesterday, but she didn't seem upset. Andy just assumed she was preparing herself for her final day. Andy has one job, and she can't fucking do it. She can't even figure out what she did wrong. It had been a good day in her book.

Oriana sighs. "Yesterday. You refused to let me do my share of the work. It was frustrating, but I'm not sure I had a right to be frustrated."

"Oh," breathes Andy. That never occurred to her. "I didn't even notice."

"Were you not mocking me for being too weak to assist when you thanked me for my help?"

"Of course not."

Ava lets out a loud snore from the living room.

"Hang on," mutters Andy. The last thing they need is to wake Ava up and get another lecture. She turns off the stove. Breakfast is ready anyway. She dumps everything onto plates and puts foil over them. She nods for Oriana to follow her to the front porch.

Andy stations them in a corner away from any windows. "Start from the beginning," she says. "I thought we had a good time yesterday."

Oriana sighs. "I know it's not my place to contradict a human, but you and your family insist that I am in some way equal. I do not understand the extent of my equality and that is sometimes frustrating." She crosses her arms and looks down at the floor.

Andy's a shitty caretaker.

"I also suppose it was upsetting to be treated like I am fragile and damaged—too damaged to be useful."

"I don't think you're damaged," says Andy quickly. She's flying blind trying to fix this, so she starts with the things that sound the worst. "You *are* equal to me, in every way. Is that why you didn't argue with me? You thought you didn't have the right?"

"No, I—I'm not sure, actually."

"You're free to argue with me any time you want. It doesn't mean I won't argue back, but that's what people do when they're, you know, when they...um...when they're...When people spend a lot of time together."

Oriana curls her wings around her shoulders like she's embarrassed or insecure about something. "I'm not sure my anger was justified."

"Doesn't matter. If I know you're mad, I can talk to you and we can figure it out together. I didn't even know you were mad yesterday."

"I broke Rule Three," says Oriana quietly.

Andy only remembers Rule One: don't touch Oriana. "What's Rule Three?"

"No stewing."

Andy laughs. "I break that rule a lot."

She smiles and looks up slightly. "I am sorry I reacted so poorly."

"You keep saying that. What did you do? I don't get what you're apologizing for."

"For upsetting you. I told you, I did it on purpose. I knew asking about your mother would upset you and I did it deliberately."

Andy overreacted yesterday. She shouldn't have spaced out. She shouldn't have gotten so upset, shouldn't be so sensitive. "Ana, I say things just to piss people off all the time. It's not a big deal."

"But I did not 'piss you off.'" She makes air quotes around Andy's words. "I hurt your feelings. I caused you grief."

Andy rolls her eyes. "Life caused me grief, not you. Besides, you were nice about it at the end. I guess you weren't mad anymore?"

"I was concerned when you stopped responding."

Andy rubs the back of her neck. "Point is, if I piss you off, you tell me. We might argue, but that's okay. And if you think I'm being a dumbass, you just tell Ava and she'll straighten us out."

"All right. I am sorry I was vindictive instead of honest."

"It's okay. I'm sorry I made you feel like you weren't useful or equal. I was worried you'd get hurt but you're strong and I was stupid."

"Our friendship is still intact?"

"Of course." It takes all her restraint to stay where she is instead of stepping forward to comfort Oriana. She looks so vulnerable. "Of course, it is." Andy hopes her words are comforting enough.

Oriana watches her. There is so much hidden behind the surface and Andy aches to know more. She clenches her hands into fists at her side to keep herself from reaching out.

Oriana looks down at Andy's hands. "You have my permission."

Andy's an open fucking book. She can't help herself. She raises one hand slowly, giving Oriana time to change her mind.

She brushes a lock of dark hair away from Oriana's face. That's a safe move. They've established face-touching is all right.

Surprisingly, Oriana mimics the motion.

Andy could stay here, exactly like this forever. "So, this isn't weird for you, is it?"

"It is new, but many normal human interactions are new to me."

"Right." She drops her hand. Oriana doesn't know what she's doing. She doesn't know the effect she has on Andy. She thinks this is normal. Andy's teaching her the wrong shit. She wishes Faith would hurry up and come back.

Oriana drops her hand too.

"We should wake up Ava before breakfast gets cold," says Andy.

Oriana nods and follows her back inside.

CHAPTER NINE

Oriana extends her good wing and flexes the muscles in the other. She extends it slowly. The joints are stiff from disuse. She opens it and for the first time in years, both wings are outstretched behind her.

Andy is staring, eyes wide.

Ava smiles at her. "Faith says you have to stay grounded until she gets back." It's a warning and a reminder. "I'd appreciate it if you would resist the urge to fly for a few more days. I don't want to explain to Dr. Black why I let her patient overexert herself."

Oriana is only half-listening. "I understand," she says. The wind blows through her feathers and the sun warms her stiff joints. She is free.

Ava says something to Andy, then leaves.

Oriana tilts her head back to face the sun. She rolls her shoulders again. Decades. It's been decades since she felt this way. Memories that she kept sequestered in her mind gush forward. She doesn't have many, but for the moment, the good overwhelms the bad and all that matters is life as it is right now.

"Feel better?" asks Andy.

"Yes." *Better* does not begin to describe the way she feels.

"Today is your last day."

"I know."

"Are you still…Do you want—what do you want to do?"

"Fly." She lowers her head to face Andy. "You were right. I no longer want to die." She retracts her wings, then flares them out again. She feels strong, *is* strong. She is stronger than her captor. An old power surges through her veins. It's what humans call magic. It's never been this dynamic. For the first time, she feels like an angel. Her life is suddenly heavy with potential and purpose.

"Are you going to leave?"

"I believe my owner has captured another angel. He was looking for a male to breed with me." She told Tristan this information and expected him to tell the others, but Andy looks surprised. Perhaps Tristan kept her secrets. "I cannot allow myself to become complacent while another angel suffers at his hands."

She doesn't realize her plan until she says it aloud. Now that she is strong, she has a responsibility. She can help. She must help. It is selfish for her to waste away and wait for death when she has this potential.

Andy knew—must have known—this would happen.

"You can't take him on alone."

"I can. I was a child when he captured me. As I grew, he kept me in a weakened state. I am stronger than I've ever been, and I have nothing to lose."

"I don't…"

Andy doesn't want her to leave. They are friends.

Oriana doesn't want to leave Andy either, but she must do this alone. "This is justice. I need to do it."

"I'll go with you."

"You can't. Would you want me to assist you while you fought the demon who killed your parents?"

"That's different. That's personal. It's a family issue."

"This is personal for me. I need to do this alone—for my family and my dignity." She hopes Andy will understand.

"Will you come back?"

Since Oriana is going to kill the man who murdered her family, she's not sure if it will impact Andy's feelings for her. "If I am still welcome."

"You better come back. You'll always be welcome here. No matter what."

Oriana realizes she wants to return. She wants to see these people again. She wants to see Andy again. "I would like to leave now, before Ava finds a way to keep me grounded."

Andy clenches her jaw like she wants to say something but is stopping herself. Oriana recognizes that look. She moves forward and so does Andy. She rests a hand on Andy's cheek and hopes the gesture is still comforting.

"I do not want Ava or Faith to be angry with you for letting me go," she says quietly. "I will be back soon." She lets the fragile tendrils of her power seep from her skin and into Andy. "I'm sorry."

Andy's eyes roll back and Oriana catches her as her knees buckle. She lowers Andy into the grass in a position she hopes is not uncomfortable. She does not have time to linger. She spreads her wings, stretches them toward the sky, and takes off.

* * *

It took her almost twelve hours to fly here. It's slow for an angel, but she didn't crash so she considers it a success.

The old house is abandoned. Oriana stands in the living room, a place she never saw when she lived here. She has not entered the silo yet. A twisted little part of her is afraid it will feel like home. She twirls a white feather between her fingers.

She holds the feather against her chest as though it will give her strength. She forces herself to enter her kidnapper's bedroom. When she sees them, she stops. Her father's wings glitter in the sunlight that pours though the window. They are spread as wide as the room will allow, with wire protruding from between the feathers, so they hang on the wall.

Oriana raises a trembling hand as she approaches. She strokes the long primary feathers. They are dusty, but still soft. The trapper must have cared for them. She undoes the wires and hooks and pins that hold the wings to the wall. She works quickly. Once her growing rage erupts, Oriana will not be able to be gentle.

When the wings are free, she folds them at their joints, surprised and sickened to find they still bend. She carries them from the house and sets them on a blanket she has spread out in the front yard. She places the white feather with a pile of other feathers, a small monument to her fallen kin.

She returns to the house. Once she is certain there is nothing left to save, she begins to destroy. Her fury blinds her as she breaks and throws the trapper's possessions. She creates a pile of what she hopes are things he loved—pictures, papers, keepsakes—and tosses a match onto the heap.

The flame does not explode in the satisfying way Oriana hoped it would, but that doesn't matter. She watches, making sure the flame will grow large enough to sustain itself, then she leaves.

She goes to the silo. She knows she needs to be quick. The smoke will attract attention eventually. The fire is her excuse not to linger. She should have gone to her cage first, but when she saw the state of the property, she knew the trapper had not been there for a while. She knew there was no one to rescue. Now it's just Oriana alone with her thoughts.

She tugs the door open, braced for the onslaught of memories, but nothing happens. The smell is familiar. The interior is familiar, though she rarely saw it with this much light. The door was never open very long. Some natural light managed to get in, through narrow openings at the top, but it was never enough to illuminate the entire silo. Her life was lived in shadows.

She goes inside and runs her fingers over a stain on the wall. She's certain it's her blood. It's a remnant of some lesson Oriana never learned. She finds the worn patch of dirt where she used to sleep and sits down. She shifts her wings as she sits. The new freedom is surreal to experience in this place. She forces herself to cycle through memories. They come in slow, oozing phases. Every day was the same in this place. Her memories bleed together to form one long, endless nightmare.

She remembers starving, dehydration, and fear. She remembers the trapper. Sometimes he would come into her cage with tears in his eyes. She never knew what triggered his emotions, but she knew how he'd calm himself. He'd rage against her until his knuckles were bloody and they were both exhausted.

An explosion echoes through the silo. The fire must have reached the gunpowder. It will reach the cage soon. Yet, she doesn't move. The air is thick with the ghosts of her past. She lays down in the dirt. It was less than a month ago that Faith and Ava found her like this. She was delirious, hungry, and broken. Since they found her, she's become someone her former self would never recognize.

The silo is getting warmer. She can smell the smoke and hear the crackling of flames as the fire approaches. She doesn't move. The fire has reached the cage. She can see the flames. She waits. A part of her needs to die here.

Another explosion from the house fuels the fire. Heat surrounds her. Oriana closes her eyes, breathing in smoke and ash. She stays until the fire engulfs her. It scorches her feathers and blisters her skin, but she heals almost as fast as the fire burns.

Once the pain begins to seep to her bones, she stands and walks to the center of the prison. The smoke stings her eyes as she watches her home—her cell—warp around her. She embraces the pain. As the fire claws at her skin, her power works to repair it. She can feel her feathers burn, then repair. She burns until the shell of her old body is gone and then steps forward from the flames.

Her skin smokes and hisses as she collects what is left of the ones who died here. She wraps the feathers securely in the large blanket along with her father's wings. She leaves the house and silo to burn and does not look back.

CHAPTER TEN

Andy wakes up in her bed in Ava's house. It takes a second for her to remember where she is. Oriana must have knocked her out. Ava must have dragged her inside. She sits up and swings her legs over the side of the bed. She's dizzy. Ava's on the phone downstairs so Andy follows the sound of her voice.

Ava must hear her coming down the stairs. "She's awake. I'll meet you there." She hangs up.

"Was that Faith?"

"Yeah. She and Tristan are about to take off. They're on a flight to Seattle. I'm going to meet them at the place where we found Oriana."

"How long was I out?"

"Long enough to give Oriana a head start."

"She went back."

"No shit."

"She's worried her kidnapper might be holding another angel."

"I know, and I know you've been covering for her, and I know why. You're going to wait here in case she comes back, but I've got to get going."

"I'm coming too."

"What did I just say?"

"You might need backup."

"I've got backup, *if* I need it."

Ava grabs a bag from the living room and heads outside. Andy follows her to her pickup.

"I told Faith you deleted that email," says Ava. "She hadn't deleted the files yet, so she sent it to me. I was pissed at first, because there's shit on there I needed to know. But then I saw you two out by the fence the other day…" Ava tosses her bag into the back of the truck. "The point is I'm not mad. You made a friend and that's good for you. It's probably good for both of you."

Andy doesn't say anything.

"I'm not mad. I'm frustrated, but I'm not mad." She glances at Andy. "Say something, don't leave me talking to myself."

Andy opens and closes her mouth a few times, but nothing comes out.

"Jesus Christ! You're speechless. I'm going to remember this. Andy Black is fucking speechless."

"She knocked me out." That's it. That's all she's got.

"I know."

"She didn't want you to get mad at me for letting her go."

"Guess she likes you. I haven't told Faith about your relationship."

"It's not a relationship."

Ava shoots Andy a sideways glance. "Well, whatever it is, I haven't told your sister. But I think it's important that you tell her. She'll be supportive. You know how Faith is."

Andy covers her face with one hand. She's fighting nausea, embarrassment, and worry. For once she finds herself wishing she was back in bed with her nightmares. "There's nothing to tell," she says finally. "We're friends, I guess."

"Considering you're *you*, that's something to tell." She chuckles to herself. "So, what's Oriana's plan? Did she give you details?"

"No."

Ava tries to dig for more information but Andy can't help her. At this point, everyone knows as much as she does. She's not even sure Oriana went in with a plan.

Ava leaves, and she doesn't seem entirely convinced that Andy's telling her the whole story.

Andy goes back inside to wait. She spends the first few hours in Ava's office looking for information on the man who was holding Oriana. She finds a few notes and figures the rest must be in Ava's room. She spends the rest of the day digging through things she's not supposed to touch and another hour trying to crack the code on the safe unsuccessfully. Andy figures she probably took the important stuff with her anyway. Frustrated, she goes upstairs and flops down on her bed. It's dark outside. She doesn't mean to fall asleep.

She dreams of her home—of her parents and Faith—of the demon who destroyed their lives.

It's early when she wakes. The sun is just beginning to creep through the curtains. The rays are enough to give away the silhouette of someone standing in the doorway. The outline isn't human. Andy recognizes Oriana's wings first.

"Hello, Andy." Her voice is hoarse and quiet.

Andy gets out of bed. As she approaches, she smells smoke.

Oriana is naked and covered in ash. Her wings are matted with gray flecks and her body is red and black. Her body is too covered in grime to pick out injuries. If that son of a bitch hurt Oriana, Andy's going to kill him. Andy might kill him anyway.

"What happened?"

"He wasn't there, so I destroyed his home."

Andy moves in closer and reaches out to touch Oriana. "You're hurt."

Oriana holds up both arms for Andy to inspect her. She's covered in minor burns. "These will heal quickly."

"Can you make it to the basement? What we need is already down there."

"Yes."

She doesn't look steady. Andy goes ahead of her down the stairs, prepared to brace herself to break Oriana's fall, should she stumble. Fortunately, they make it into the basement in one piece.

Andy turns on the shower and adjusts the temperature to avoid aggravating Oriana's burns. She motions for her to stand under the water. "Does the water hurt?"

"No."

Andy doesn't miss the shiver that runs through Oriana's body and into her wings. "I know it's too cold. You don't have to stay under there long. I just want to get you clean."

"The temperature is fine."

Andy rolls her eyes. "Do you need help with your wings?"

At that, both wings twitch and the feathers ruffle. Oriana turns to face Andy, her back to the water. "I—no," she stammers.

"I'll be careful. You can't reach them on your own, can you?"

She glances at her back, as though debating whether this is a task she can complete.

"I know wings are—um—personal, but I don't mind helping."

Oriana chews her bottom lip. She looks to Andy and nods slowly.

"I'll be careful. Any burns I should know about?"

She shakes her head.

Andy circles her to work on the back of the wings first. She uses her fingers instead of a cloth so she can feel for damage. She combs through the long black feathers several times to shake out the ash. She tries to be quick. Oriana stays very still for the whole ordeal. It's the second time she's had someone messing with her wings and she's no more at ease than she was when Faith did it.

By the time Andy moves to the front of the wings, she's drenched and shivering. "Almost done," says Andy. She knows Oriana must be cold too.

"All right," she murmurs. She almost looks drunk.

Humans don't touch angel wings. They are sacred, intimate, beautiful. That's why trappers keep them as trophies. Andy knows that. She's trying not to think about it right now. She buries her fingers into the feathers, working her way from the end of the wings up to Oriana's shoulder. Faith was so much more efficient when she did this.

Oriana jumps when Andy reaches the smaller, softer feathers at the base of the wings.

"Sorry."

Neither of them makes eye contact.

She finishes one wing and moves on to the other, again working her way from the end, back toward Oriana's shoulder. This time, when she jumps, Andy looks up and their eyes lock. Andy is frozen to the spot. Feathers ruffle beneath her fingers. She takes a sharp inhale. Oriana is staring into her.

Angels and demons can hypnotize humans and compel them to do things. She's not using magic, though. She's just staring and Andy can't move. They stand—motionless—under the water until Oriana blinks and her wings ruffle again.

Andy, finally able to move, finishes the wing. "Done," she says, and despite herself, she takes Oriana by the hands and pulls her out from under the spray.

She shuts off the water, grabs several towels and some clothes from the closet. Ava and Faith are prepared for everything. The shirt she selects has cutouts for wings in the back. It buttons at the back of the collar and ties at the waist so they don't have to maneuver it over her wings.

She sets the items in a stack in front of Oriana. "You should dry off and get changed," she says. "I'll be right back." She doesn't wait for Oriana to respond before leaving. She's sure Faith keeps the rec room stocked with medical supplies. It's got everything else, but Andy can't stay in there. She needs to breathe air that Oriana isn't breathing. She needs to stop thinking about her soft feathers and striking eyes.

She gives Oriana enough time to change before heading back. Andy calls out about halfway down the stairs to let her know she's coming. "Hey, Ana, you dressed?"

"Yes."

Andy enters and dumps an armful of supplies on the bed. She pulls up a stool and instructs Oriana to sit. "How are you feeling?"

"Better," she answers. Oriana doesn't have any wounds. She's healed completely from whatever happened to her.

That doesn't stop Andy from making a fuss and double-checking her for signs of injury.

"Where is Ava?"

Oops.

She forgot to tell the others Oriana was back. "Ava, Faith, and Tristan went to look for you in Washington. I've got to call them and tell them you came back."

"Tristan knew my plan. He knew where to find me, though I suppose that would be the first logical place to look anyway."

"Are you worried he ratted you out—er—told them your plan?"

"I expected him to. I didn't tell him anything secret."

"Oh." Andy's curious now. What does she consider secret?

Oriana doesn't smell like soot anymore. She smells like honey and clover and rain. The scent is subtle, but Andy is consumed by it. She turns back and puts on her best "everything's fine" face.

"Thank you for your help."

"You're welcome." She clears her throat and tries not to look at the way Oriana's wings glimmer with the remaining bits of water.

Of course, Oriana notices her looking. She follows Andy's line of sight. "I would like to go outside so my wings can dry."

"Do you want to go alone, or do you want me to go with you?"

"You trust me to go alone?"

"I trust you to do whatever you want."

"I would like to go alone. Does that offend you?"

"No, I'll call the others and tell them you're safe."

She doesn't follow her outside, but Andy does position herself by an upstairs window overlooking the pasture. She should call, but she shoots Faith a text instead.

Oriana is here. Says she destroyed the house. She's safe.

She watches the angel lay on her stomach in the grass and unfurl her wings. Andy rests her head against the warm windowpane.

Faith replies. *Yeah. We found it in ashes. We'll all head back home tomorrow.*

Andy doesn't send a response. She gets up and tosses her phone onto her bed and deliberately forgets about it. It's lunchtime.

Oriana will be hungry soon. She goes down to the kitchen and paws through Ava's fridge. Andy settles on peanut butter and jelly sandwiches—mostly because that's all she can make with what she finds. Ava's never been great about stocking up on groceries.

She takes her time making sandwiches and eating one. She's not sure how long Oriana wants to be alone. Andy decides to clean the kitchen and make a grocery list to distract herself. An hour later, she hasn't heard from Oriana. She decides that's a reasonable excuse to check on her. She takes a sandwich and a glass of water outside.

Oriana is still lying in the grass so Andy sets the plate and glass on the table outside. She struggles with herself for a moment. She should respect her space. She doesn't need to hover.

Oriana's wings twitch and begin to retract, only to extend again. The movement is not big enough to wake her, but it's still noticeable. Andy has seen angels do the same motion when they're trying to threaten their opponent. She creeps quickly, but cautiously, over to Oriana. As she suspected, she is sleeping. This must be the beginning of a nightmare. She crouches down. "Hey, Ana? Can you hear me?" She leans in closer.

Her face is twisted and tense with emotion. Her arms are folded above her head in the grass, unmoving, but her fists are clenched. Andy lets out a breath and extends her hand. She lets it rest on Oriana's cheek. Her eyes move beneath her lids and Andy's not sure if that's good or bad. She decides to try plan B.

She hums. She's quiet at first, self-conscious, but Oriana's wings move again, and she knows she has to be louder if she wants to reach her.

She starts singing. She moves her fingers through Oriana's hair. She remembers her mother. She tries to channel the tranquility her memory brings. It works. After a minute, Oriana stops twitching and relaxes. Andy lowers herself so she's lying eye-level in front of her. She's still stroking her hair, still singing softly.

Oriana's hands are resting between them. Her fists unclench and her breathing slows. She uncurls her fingers and moves her hand to rest on Andy's arm. She tilts her head to face Andy. She blinks sluggishly. "Hello."

Andy grins. "Hey." She swallows hard. "This...Is this okay?"

"Yes." Oriana trails her fingers along Andy's arm.

"You want to talk about it? Your dream? You don't have to, just...if you want to, I'll listen."

A frown ghosts across Oriana's face. "Not right now. I'd rather not spoil the moment."

"Are we having a moment?" It's a stupid question, but she needs to know if this means to Oriana what it means to her. Is Andy just comforting a friend, or is Oriana's heart also trying to beat its way out of her chest? Part of her doesn't want an answer. Part of her wants to stay like this forever, perfectly preserved in hope.

"What constitutes a moment?" asks Oriana.

Andy laughs, because of course that's the answer she gets. "Never mind. You hungry? I made you a sandwich, but it's been sitting out for a while. I'll make you a fresh one, or I could make you something else. What do you like? We don't have a lot of options, but I can get creative." She fills the air with something more mundane to keep herself from asking what she really wants to know. She's still stroking Oriana's hair and Oriana is still touching her arm.

A little crease forms between her eyebrows. "Why do you do that?"

"Do what?"

"Ask me something then change the subject."

A shiver goes through Andy. "I don't know."

Oriana stares at her, decoding her again. "I believe we are having a moment."

"I guess we are." She tries not to make it significant. Oriana doesn't know what she's saying.

"I did not have nightmares when I spent the night in your cabin," Oriana says. "I believe we had a moment then as well."

They've had this conversation before. "I didn't have nightmares either."

"And did we have a moment?"

As far as Andy can tell, she's completely serious. "Yeah, I think we did."

"And when we were mending the fence?"

"Also a moment."

Her frown fades into a smile. "Then a moment must be a period of gentleness and affection between friends."

"That's accurate." She's not going to read into the use of the words *affection* and *friends*. "You want a sandwich?"

Oriana sighs. "Yes."

Andy is reluctant to pull away, but she manages. She pushes herself to her feet then offers a hand to Oriana, which she accepts, and they return to the house.

CHAPTER ELEVEN

The day drags by lazy and peaceful. Andy makes spaghetti for dinner, and she uses teaching Oriana how to twirl the pasta as an excuse to sit close to her. She tells herself she's not a creep, but she can't shake the feeling that she's preying upon Oriana's naiveté about human interactions.

She's been toying with an idea all afternoon but doesn't have the courage to suggest it. She can't figure out how to ask Oriana to sleep in her room without sounding weird. Andy would sleep on a mat on the floor, of course. They don't need to share a bed, but being in the same room seemed to comfort both of them. Maybe that's just an excuse.

Evening arrives too soon, and she follows Oriana upstairs to their respective bedrooms.

"Andy?" Oriana pauses outside of her room and reaches into her pocket. "I thought you might need this." Oriana extends her hand to reveal Andy's flask.

"Where did you get that?" She takes it and shakes the container. It's full.

"Ava's safe."

"How?"

"I know the combination."

Andy takes a drink and holy shit it's liquid sanctuary. She licks her lips. It's not enough to kick off her normal midnight buzz, but that first burn of whiskey is a long exhale after a hard day's work.

"I know it's bad for your health. I believe I am 'enabling' you, but you helped me leave. This is the least I can do."

"Thank you." She runs her thumb over the initials "J.B." inscribed into the metal on the back of the flask. It's a security blanket—a crutch. She knows that. It was probably a crutch for Jeremy too. She takes another pull, then extends the flask to Oriana.

She frowns at it like it's a puzzle.

"Just take a sip. Don't make me drink alone." She flashes a grin usually reserved for the bartenders on lonely nights just before closing time.

Oriana accepts and takes a timid sip. She hands the flask back to Andy and seems to be concentrating on the liquid in her mouth.

"You've got to swallow it," says Andy.

She does and makes a face. "The liquid is not hot, but it burns."

"It's supposed to."

"I'd like to try more."

Andy offers her the flask again, but Oriana shakes her head. "I procured several bottles from the safe, as well as your possessions. They are in your room."

Andy whips around and pushes the door open. Oriana isn't lying. Her gear, the rest of her clothing, and car keys are sitting in the middle of her bed, along with two bottles of Ava's secret stash.

"When?"

"While you were preparing dinner."

Andy turns to face her and something in her stings. Oriana even brought up her weapons, everything from guns to holy water. Oriana must know Andy's used these things to inflict the same torture her captor inflicted on her. Still, Oriana trusts her. She shouldn't. Why would she? No one else does.

"Would you like some company while you drink?" asks Oriana.

"Yeah, please." Andy finally realizes Oriana is waiting for her to move so they can go into the room. She goes over to the bed and grabs a bottle.

Oriana eyes a spot on the edge of the bed. "May I?"

"Yeah, get comfortable."

She perches at the foot of the bed with her wings hanging onto the floor.

Andy uncorks the bottle and hands it to Oriana. "Here's to being ungrounded." She clinks her flask against the bottle and drinks.

Oriana watches her, then does the same.

"This is called a toast. You drink to commemorate something and clink your glasses together."

"Humans do this?"

"Yeah."

Oriana takes another drink, deeper than the one before. She wipes her mouth on the back of her hand and sighs like she's been holding her breath. "I would like to talk with you. You allowed me to pry into your past. It is only fair I do the same for you."

Andy tries to mask her excitement with surprise. "You don't have to, but I'll listen to anything you're willing to share."

She takes another drink, and her wings move to shelter her shoulders. "I don't know how to begin."

"How about I ask some questions and you answer if you feel like it?"

Oriana nods.

"How old were you when you were captured?" It's not the best question, but it's what she thinks to ask first.

"Eight."

It's Andy's turn to take a drink. She empties the flask. "What happened to your dad?"

A frown pulls at Oriana's lips and she drinks too. "He died." She closes her eyes, scowling at the memory. "My owner—"

"Kidnapper."

"My kidnapper...He believed he could train us to obey him." Another drink. "My father was already weakened during the capture. He..." Oriana clears her throat. "My father did not survive the training. He was strong—rebellious—but the trapper used my safety as an ultimatum and in the end, it broke him. I loved him as you loved your mother."

Andy cracks open the remaining bottle.

Oriana has a white-knuckled grip around the neck of the other one.

"I'm sorry you lost him. What was he like before?"

Oriana sighs. "Kind." She drinks. "He used to say I was just like my mother, but I like to think I was more like him." Another sigh. "I think I look like him."

"His real form or like the human he possessed?" Andy knows that was the wrong thing to ask, but she can't take it back.

Oriana clenches her jaw. "I never knew his angelic form."

Andy knows she should apologize. She needs to make this right before it gets worse, but she can't find the words. Instead, all she does is wonder if Oriana's father matches a description for a missing person.

"You think he was a monster," mutters Oriana.

"No."

"You thought I was a monster."

"I...yeah."

Oriana stares down at the bottle in her hands. "I've never been to the realm of angels. I don't know what they look like. My father was banished for loving a human. He was not a monster, but he did bad things."

"Like?"

Oriana drinks again, deep and anxious. "I'm afraid you would hate him, if you knew."

"I won't." That's not a promise Andy can keep, but she says it anyway.

"What do you know about my kind?" She leans forward. "Do you know about the war?"

"Kind of." At this point she's just relieved Oriana is still willing to talk to her. "I know angels fight demons and sometimes they come into our world and take over humans."

"Angels and demons have been at war for a long time. In your dimension, it equates to centuries." Her brow furrows. "I was too young to understand. My education comes partially from my father and partially from my own—my kidnapper. I know there is a small faction that fights, or used to fight, to protect humanity." She pauses, thinking. "Your species is weaker, therefore, some believed we have a responsibility to protect you when the war bleeds into your world." Oriana bites her lip. "The majority, however, use human bodies to either flee the war and start a new life, or to simply feed off their energy to become stronger." She's not making eye contact anymore. "I very much want to believe that my father fought to save your kind."

"But?" Andy's not sure if she said that out loud.

"But he died before I was old enough to hear his story." Oriana's eyes are glassy.

Andy's not sure if it's liquor or emotion.

"He left his home to be with my mother," she whispers. "He loved her. I killed her. She was the first human I killed. He could not return home because I was too human, and he could not live as a human because I am not human enough." Oriana finally looks up at Andy again. "As I understand it, most of mankind does not know we exist."

Andy nods. Very few know the truth.

"He killed people to keep me safe. When we were finally captured, he was still injured from an earlier fight. The trapper took me first, threatened me, and my father surrendered."

Andy doesn't know how to form her next question. Oriana said her mother was the *first* human life she took. Were there others?

"I know why you kill us," says Oriana. "In some respect, we are monsters. We are creatures of death and destruction. We take your loved ones and use them for our own gain. Angels and demons cannot live in your world without a human body. You sacrifice for our benefit." Tears begin rolling down her cheeks. "The strong have a duty to defend the weak. I was weak for so long. I thought only of defending myself." She takes another drink. "I never tried to save them."

Andy sets her own bottle on the bedside table, then leans in to extract the other one. Without taking her eyes off Oriana, Andy pulls the whiskey away and sets it on the table. "Save who?"

Oriana doesn't answer. She leans forward, head in her hands, trembling, and Andy crawls over to sit beside her. Oriana flinches but doesn't move away. She turns to Andy, a pleading look in her eyes. "He brought them into the cage, they were so broken, and I just watched them die. He'd tell me their stories before he did it—who they were and what took them—and I just watched."

Andy doesn't know what to say, so she moves a strand of hair from Oriana's face.

"You don't understand what I'm saying, do you?"

Andy doesn't, but at the same time, she doesn't care. Oriana is hurting. That's all she cares about.

"He brought in humans, like you and your family. They were possessed, then abandoned. They'd gone mad. They begged for help and I did nothing. He gave me a chance to save them, and I just listened until they stopped screaming."

Andy goes for broke and carefully tugs Oriana into her arms. "It's okay, Ana," she whispers. "It wasn't your fault."

Oriana cries, but she lets Andy hold her. "I don't deserve this."

Andy pulls Oriana's head down to rest against her shoulder, then she leans in and presses a kiss against her temple. "I don't deserve this either."

Oriana is quiet, but still shaking. Andy argues with herself for a moment. She has an idea that will either help or hurt. Oriana seems so distraught she decides to risk it.

Andy pulls away from her and reaches for the bag containing the acid. Most of her weapons are still on the bed where Oriana left them. She reaches into the bag and pulls out a handful of feathers. She's holding around twenty and that's not even her total body count. She has nothing to show for the ones whose wings disappeared before she had a chance to grab a trophy.

She extends her hand to Oriana. "I'm bad too," she mutters.

Oriana looks from Andy to the feathers for a moment, before taking them into her own hands. She runs her fingers over the frayed places. Her lips are parted, but she's not speaking.

"I never asked if they were trying to save us. Plenty of them begged." Her voice cracks and she tries again. "They begged me to let them go and I didn't."

Oriana still isn't speaking. She pulls away from Andy again, feathers clutched to her chest, gets off the bed, and leaves the room.

Andy doesn't go after her. She knew it was a risk. She knew better than to hope for forgiveness. She's crying and she's not sure why. At least Oriana is angry instead of depressed. Andy would give anything to never see that helpless look on her face again.

Something scrapes against the hallway floor and Andy starts when she sees Oriana standing at her door again. She's clutching something. "Will you help me?" she asks. "There's more outside at the far end of the field."

Andy scrambles from the bed and Oriana takes a step back into the hall. "The feathers are in the blanket," she says.

Andy steps out of the room and realizes the bundle in Oriana's arms is too big to just hold the feathers she just gave her. She feels a chill again and realizes these must have come from the other trapper's house.

"What are we doing?" asks Andy.

"I'd like to burn these. Your feathers are wrapped separately, if you wish to keep them."

"No. Hang on." She goes back to her room and pockets Jeremy's flask before returning to the hall. "Okay. I'm ready." She's not sure if it's the liquor talking, but this feels right. She follows Oriana outside and they search for a place to build the fire.

They settle on a dusty section of the unpaved road and work quickly to create a pit. Oriana creates a rock barrier. She's stronger and faster than Andy, so Andy busies herself with collecting wood. In the center of the pit, she sets Jeremy's flask. Oriana watches her but doesn't say anything. Andy retrieves the lighter fluid while Oriana begins arranging feathers among the wood.

"I'll be right back," says Oriana. She stretches her wings and takes off, leaving Andy in a dust cloud.

Andy blinks and watches Oriana's silhouette glide against the starry sky. She flies to the far end of the pasture and returns with something huge in her arms. When she lands, Andy realizes she's carrying a pair of wings. They must have been her father's. She steps to the stack of wood and feathers and places the wings, folded, among the logs.

Andy douses the pyre until it reeks of gas. She knows she's had too much to drink to do this safely. She hopes the fire will burn hot enough to destroy everything. She strikes a match and throws it into the pile.

Oriana grabs her around the waist and pulls her back as the pyre explodes. For a moment, she's cocooned in darkness, shielded from the heat by Oriana's wings. She doesn't touch them and stays very still where she is pressed close to Oriana's body.

Oriana opens her wings.

The flames lick against the sky in an inferno towering at least twenty feet. The heat stings Andy's face where she stands, still in Oriana's arms. Oriana stares into the flames until Andy pulls her away so they can sit in the grass and watch their memories burn.

Later, Oriana kneels by the fire and the blaze turns from orange to white.

"What are you doing?" asks Andy.

"Helping it along."

They keep watch through the night in a strange reverence. In the morning, the fire is still glowing and all that remains are fragments of bone and a warped scrap of metal. They extinguish the coals and then bury the whole thing, erasing all evidence that the pit ever existed.

When Andy finally returns to her room to sleep, Oriana follows. They curl together in bed without a word, and Oriana rests against Andy's chest, one wing draped over their bodies.

CHAPTER TWELVE

Oriana steps beneath the water of the rec room shower as it is the only shower that can accommodate her wings. She turns her face up into the spray from the shower. Oriana didn't dream last night. She's not sure if it was Andy's warm presence or her snoring that kept her nightmares at bay. She's grateful either way.

She can't remember much about last night. She remembers fragments of confessions, the funeral pyre, and Andy. She scrubs herself of the smell of soot for the second day in a row. She shuts off the water and dries off as much as she can before returning upstairs.

She goes to Andy's room, unsure if she's allowed to return to the bed since she left. Andy has one arm thrown over the spot where Oriana was laying and she's scowling in her sleep. Oriana decides she can return to her spot if she doesn't disturb Andy. She crawls carefully into the bed and settles back into place with her head against Andy's chest.

Andy instantly curls into her, nuzzling her face into Oriana's hair. She rests a hand on Andy's chest and Andy takes it in her own, pressing it into her T-shirt. Oriana cannot help but grin up at the sleeping human. She watches her until she begins to stir. She pulls away just enough for Andy to comfortably get out of bed.

Andy wakes up several minutes later and leaves the room. When she comes back, she returns to her spot in the bed, just as Oriana did. Andy reaches out and brushes her fingers over Oriana's forehead.

Presumably, it's all right that Oriana came back if Andy did the same. Rules do not change with Andy. She is constant. She does not contradict herself. She is strong and she has allowed Oriana to become stronger. She is also fragile, but not so fragile Oriana can break her. She is patient and Oriana is safe with her. Andy pets her hair. It's still wet and she probably knows Oriana is awake.

"You are a heavy sleeper," says Oriana, opening one eye to watch her.

Andy pulls her hand away. "I thought you were still asleep."

"I woke up an hour ago."

"You took a shower?"

"I did." Oriana looks to Andy and bites her lip. There is more space between them. "I came back to wake you, but you were sleeping so peacefully. Do you mind that I came back to bed?"

Andy grins and pulls Oriana back into her arms. "I'm glad you came back." She runs her fingers along Oriana's jaw and Oriana closes her eyes, drinking in the softness of the touch.

"Is this okay?"

"Yes."

She's having trouble breathing, but she's not upset. She trusts Andy even though she knows she shouldn't. She knows better. She knows now that Andy has her weapons, she's likely to leave. She knows humans are not always what they seem. None of that stops her from wanting to hold this human close forever.

"Still okay?" asks Andy.

Oriana nods. She is fine. The panic slithering through her body is a relic of the past. Andy's been so kind to Oriana. At the very least she owes Andy her trust.

"What are you thinking?" whispers Andy.

"I'm not sure."

"You're thinking I'm a killer. You gave me my gear back as a test."

"No," Oriana lies. "I trust you."

"You don't have to trust me."

"But you've been so kind." Humans expect something in exchange for kindness. It doesn't anger Oriana the way it used to.

"I'm trying to earn your trust. Doesn't mean you have to give it to me."

"You trust me," says Oriana. She's done nothing to *earn* Andy's trust. "We've been conditioned for violence against each other and yet you trust me."

Andy grins. "I'm working on it."

Maybe Oriana is working on it, too. Maybe trust is an action, not a reward for civility. Maybe she can "work on" trusting Andy.

"How about we get some breakfast?" asks Andy.

Oriana looks up at her. She pushes herself up then kisses Andy's cheek. She can hear the steady thump of Andy's heartbeat. "Your heart…it's racing."

"Yeah."

"I don't want breakfast yet."

"Okay."

Oriana bites back a smile. She's not even using her power and Andy is completely captivated. She wonders what else will make Andy's heart beat faster. She brushes her fingertips over Andy's lips. "Are you all right?"

"Yeah."

Something warm blooms in Oriana's chest. "I trust you." She leans down and kisses Andy's lips as gently as she can.

Electricity is the only way to describe what she's feeling now. There's more to this, she's vaguely aware. What else did she miss during her captivity? She needs to know what else makes her skin itch and her body crave more.

The touch feeds a famine Oriana did not realize existed. "How long before the others return?" she asks. She knows this—whatever this is—won't last forever. Andy's job taking care of her is over. She'll leave soon.

"Probably tomorrow afternoon."

Andy can leave when they return. She cups Andy's face in her hands, making sure she has her full attention. "Will you come back?" She needs an answer, and she wants Andy to know she knows what she's thinking.

"Am I going somewhere?"

"At some point you will return to your job."

"Don't worry about that now."

"I'm not worried. It is an inevitability, one I understand very well. I was just wondering if you will come back here when you are done."

"Yes."

"Please answer honestly."

Andy closes her eyes and grimaces. "I don't know. What about you?"

Oriana hadn't considered that. She will leave again to find the trapper, and when she does? Then what? Where will she go? She's not sure why she came back after she burned the house. Her life cannot revolve around another human. She must make her decision independent of Andy.

After only a few days with her freedom, she's already tied to another human, and this time she did it to herself. She's never lived without someone controlling her. Andy is obviously more caring than controlling, but Oriana is still not acting independently. She's not even sure if she can. She's traded someone else's cage for someone else's home.

She realizes she's pulled away from Andy and curled into herself at the foot of the bed. Her knees are tucked to her chest with her arms around them like a child. She's not strong, and she never will be if she stays. Destroying the cage should have helped.

Andy is sitting across the bed with a hand outstretched. "What did I do?"

Oriana presses her forehead to her knees. She cannot make herself stop thinking.

"Ana?" asks Andy. "What did I do?" Then, after a moment, she continues, "It's okay. I went too fast. That's not your fault. That's on me."

"I'm all right," Oriana mutters into her knees. "I am overcome with emotion. I can't make it stop."

Andy laughs. "That's usually when I start drinking."

Oriana looks up at her. "You can't make it stop either?"

Andy shakes her head. "Ava keeps saying I need to talk it out."

Oriana nods. "That was Tristan's advice to me as well."

Andy sighs. "Do you want to talk about what just happened?"

"No, but I can tell I've confused you, so it only seems fair that we talk."

Andy shakes her head. "Don't worry about me. What do you want to do? What do you need right now?"

Oriana rests her head on her knees again. "I don't know," she groans.

She wants to leave. She wants to run and prove she can be a part of this world. She knows that's never going to happen. She's too much for one world and not enough for the other. She's trapped in her own personal hell waiting for someone to want her.

And then there's Andy. There is one human who clearly wants her, but not enough to leave her world behind to join Oriana in limbo. Oriana can't ask that of her, it isn't fair to want Andy to suffer alongside her.

"Hey, Ana?"

"What?"

"You know you don't have to stay here, right?"

"I know." She shouldn't stay. She should leave before whatever this is gets worse.

"I'm not sure what to do here."

"I liked laying with you."

"I liked that, too. We could do it again."

Oriana looks at her. "Why? Will it help? Is it a human thing?"

"I don't know if it will help, but it is something humans do when they feel bad. Sometimes. I don't know."

Oriana doesn't miss that Andy says "they" instead of "we." She excludes herself. Has she always done that?

"I'm bad at this," Andy continues. "Faith would know what to do, hell, so would Tristan and Ava." She sighs and runs her hand though her hair. "Honestly, I'm the last person you should be alone with."

Oriana frowns as she moves from the edge of the bed. She crawls to Andy and pushes her onto the mattress. She tucks herself into the crook of Andy's arm and rests her head on Andy's chest and listens to her heart. She counts the steady rhythm and tries to remember the peace she felt when she first woke up.

Andy makes something called "stir-fry" for dinner. She seems distracted as she buzzes around the kitchen, so Oriana stays quiet.

She'd spent the afternoon outside. She'd flown from Ava's property to a nearby pond to remind herself she's free and then made a conscious decision to go back.

She watches as Andy prepares two plates and takes a seat at the table. Oriana thanks her for dinner and tries to find a way to explain herself.

Across the table, Andy clears her throat and Oriana looks up at her.

"I think we need to talk about us," says Andy.

"All right," agrees Oriana, slightly relieved that Andy is taking the initiative on the topic.

Andy exhales. She's nervous. "Do you know the difference between…Do you know how sometimes people have different kinds of relationships and stuff?"

It takes Oriana a minute to sort out what Andy is trying to say.

"Let me try again. Do you know the difference between romantic feelings and friend feelings?"

"Oh, yes. I think I have a basic grasp of both feelings. What I feel for you is romantic and what I feel for Ava is friendship." She knows about these feelings in theory and is working on using them in practice.

"Okay, so I have romantic feelings for you too, but I think that's bad."

Oriana's breath catches in her chest. "Because I'm a monster."

"No," says Andy quickly.

Oriana tries to relax but this is not the conversation she expected.

"No," repeats Andy. "You're not a monster. I'm taking advantage of you. I manipulated you. You like me because you don't know any better. I'm a trapper. You can't possibly have feelings for a trapper. This is—there's a term for this—I think it's like Stockholm syndrome. Tristan would know—"

"You think I'm sick and that's why I like you?"

Does Andy think she's so easily manipulated? Is she equating Oriana's feelings with some kind of mental illness? Or does she think Oriana is so inexperienced and simpleminded that she doesn't know her own feelings?

"I think you're used to trappers and that's why I feel familiar, but you don't realize that you don't like me as a person, you like that I'm a trapper because that's what you know."

Oriana's entire body is numb. She can't speak for the rage constricting her thoughts. She's worked so hard to trust Andy, to understand Andy and her family. "You think I'm..." She pauses, looking for the right word. "...stupid?"

"No! Not at all."

Proof. Andy needs proof. It's not enough for Oriana to return her weapons, or share her secrets, or offer Andy a bond she's never offered anyone else. Andy thinks she is just a stupid monster. Andy is the all-knowing, all-powerful human who knows what's best for her stupid little pet.

Maybe she's right. Maybe Oriana can never be free. Maybe she's better off owned. She's standing with both hands braced against the table, but she doesn't remember leaving her seat. She glares at Andy, then leaves. She's too angry to make sense of what she's thinking and feeling. She needs to be alone.

CHAPTER THIRTEEN

Oriana flies over the trees. She spent the night sitting on the roof of the house. She's not as angry as she was last night. Andy's behavior was out of character. Then again, people are not always what they seem. Either Andy does not understand her the way Oriana thought, or they are having difficulty communicating.

After Andy went to bed, Oriana used Ava's computer to look up "Stockholm syndrome" and decided it was not something that applied to her. She also researched other mental disorders and found several that could apply to both her and Andy.

Tristan is due to arrive today. They need to sit down and talk with him. Oriana wants to understand and he is the expert. Oriana also read about romantic relationships and proper relationship maintenance. Andy's accusation that Oriana didn't understand her own feelings was partially true. That was part of the reason she got upset, but she was not able to communicate that at the time. She read that it was not uncommon for two people to need a moderator to listen to their stories and help them find common ground. It would be easier to run, but whatever she has with Andy deserves a second chance.

Oriana hears a car below her. They're early.

She dives down to meet them and follows them up the driveway. They are all traveling in Ava's truck. Faith gets out first and stares, mouth agape, at Oriana's wings. "You're healed. Can I look at your wing? I mean, you're flying so I guess it works, but damn. That was fast. Is that an angel thing? It's got to be. Do you know how it works?"

Tristan steps up behind her. "She means, 'Hello and it's nice to see you again.'"

"Right," stammers Faith. "I just—wow—I've never seen a recovery time like that. And your scars are gone."

"I burned them off."

"You can do that?" asks Faith.

"Why did you do that?" asks Tristan. He's just as wide-eyed as his wife.

"I was attempting to cleanse myself of my past. Actually, Tristan, when you have a moment, I'd like to speak with you."

"You *want* to speak with me?"

"Yes. I assume you are familiar with emotional conflicts."

"Yeah," he says. "We can talk whenever you want." He and Faith are both grinning.

Oriana isn't sure what she's done to make them so happy, but she's got a strange warm feeling in her chest.

"Is Andy inside?" asks Ava. She shoulders her bag and shuts the door to the truck.

"I believe so. I've been out flying for a while." She leaves out the fight. That seems like something she and Andy should explain together.

"I'll go get her," says Faith.

"We'll be in the kitchen," says Ava. "I'm starving."

"Andy made stir-fry last night," says Oriana. "There are leftovers."

"Andy cooked?" asks Ava. "I didn't know she knew how to turn on the stove."

Oriana hums. "She's very good at it."

They go to the kitchen and Tristan and Ava sample the leftover food, seemingly surprised to find the meal is good.

Faith and Andy enter the kitchen a few minutes later. Oriana sees Andy out of the corner of her eye and a new and unexpected wave of anger sweeps over her. She can't even bring herself to make eye contact.

"So," says Ava, "how've things been going with you two?" Her eyebrows are raised as though there is a more significant meaning to her words.

"Really good," answers Andy.

If Andy is going to lie, then Oriana will lie too. "My condition is much improved."

"You seem much stronger," says Tristan.

"I am." She was not prepared to get angry again.

The room grows uncomfortably quiet, and Oriana is aware that she and Andy are the main focus. It makes her uneasy.

"Oriana, Andy, let's go upstairs," says Ava.

"What's going on?" asks Tristan.

Oriana and Andy answer in unison. "Nothing."

"Did I miss something?" asks Faith.

"Ana?" asks Andy. "Can I talk to you alone?"

If she wanted to talk alone, she should have reached out last night. It's too late for that now.

"I think we should both talk to Tristan," says Oriana.

"Andy?" asks Faith.

Oriana hears Andy's heart rate increase and she's standing very still. She's searching for a way out.

"I kissed her," says Andy, suddenly.

Oriana shakes her head because Andy's had an entire night to think this through and figure out what went wrong. "That is *not* why I'm angry," she says, perhaps more forcefully than necessary.

"Then why the fuck did you leave?" snaps Andy.

"You said I have Stockholm syndrome," says Oriana, though that's not exactly why she's mad either.

"You don't even know what that is."

"I looked it up on Ava's computer."

"You don't know how to use a computer."

"Yes, I do. Faith showed me."

"You were mad before you looked it up. You were mad when we woke up. Hell, you were mad when we went to bed."

"If you're keeping track on my anger, Andy, then you should know I've been mad for decades."

"Ladies," shouts Ava, "do you want to talk about this, or do you want to see who draws first blood?"

"What the hell did we miss?" mutters Tristan. "Are you guys together?"

"Ask Andy," spits Oriana. "She's more than willing to speak for me, since I'm just a stupid monster."

"That's *not* what I said!" She crosses her arms. "We're not together. Oriana is just confused. I did things I shouldn't have done, and she doesn't understand, and I just want to fucking apologize so I can leave and not have to bother with this shit anymore."

That's it. That's what Oriana needed to know. Andy really does think she's a stupid monster.

"If you belittle my understanding of this world one more time," growls Oriana. It's easier to threaten than think about the fact that Andy wants to leave, that Oriana isn't and never will be enough. Maybe Andy is right. Maybe Oriana is confused. She thought Andy cared for her.

"You'll what?" snaps Andy.

Faith intervenes and stands between them with her back to Oriana. "What the fuck?" she asks Andy. "Start from the beginning."

Tristan begins to pull Oriana out of the room, but she doesn't move.

"No," she says. "I want to hear what Andy has to say."

She needs to know how much of this was a lie. Maybe Andy wasn't trying to insult her. Maybe she was trying to confess.

Andy gives a version of the events leading up to their fight. Oriana fills in a few minor details.

"Is that accurate?" Ava asks, once Andy is finished.

"Yes, though Andy's account presumes I was not an equal player."

"Were you?" asks Tristan.

"Yes."

Andy begins to back away from them. She's very pale. "I'm sorry, Faith."

"It's okay."

"I fucked up."

"We can fix it," says Faith.

Andy keeps moving back toward the doorway, and Faith moves to stop her, but Ava says to let her go.

It's probably for the best. Andy is shutting down. They're not going to get anything from her right now, though that was not the reaction Oriana expected. Andy leaves and the others turn to her.

"We'll give her a few minutes to cool off," says Ava, "then I'll talk to her. In the meantime, how are you holding up?"

"I'm all right," answers Oriana, arms firmly crossed. "I would still like to speak with Tristan at some point."

"Want to talk now?" asks Tristan.

Oriana nods. Her research on the computer suggested she should seek counsel from a trained professional. "Can we take a walk?"

"Of course," he answers.

They leave Faith and Ava in the kitchen. Tristan lets Oriana begin the conversation. She waits until they are well away from the house before she speaks. "I have too many emotions."

"That's not necessarily a bad thing."

"It feels bad."

"How so?"

"It makes it difficult to understand what I'm feeling." Oriana doesn't think that makes sense, but she read it was better to be honest.

"Can you tell me what you're feeling now?"

Oriana thinks for a minute. "Angry. Frustrated. Disappointed."

"What are you angry about?"

"I don't know." She's angry at a million different things.

"Are you angry with Andy?"

"Yes, but it's not just her. It's—" She's cut off by the sound of an engine. Without a second thought, she spreads her wings and shoots into the sky. Andy's truck is speeding away from the house and Faith and Ava are running after it. Oriana perches on the roof of the house as the vehicle disappears in a cloud of dust. She doesn't follow. She lets Andy go.

CHAPTER FOURTEEN

Andy stops driving after eight hours. She zones out and follows the road out of town and somewhere unfamiliar. She stops at a rest area, locks her doors and sits with her gun in her lap.

A phone rings from the bag in the passenger seat. The same ring has been haunting her since she stopped for gas three hours ago. Three missed calls. She glares at the bag for a minute, then opens it. Jeremy's phone is illuminated and ringing. She recognizes the number. It's the same one that's been calling without leaving a message. She knows she has to do this eventually. It's part of her job. She answers the phone.

"Jeremy?" asks the caller, before Andy can speak.

"Andy."

"I need to talk to your dad. This is Christian. Tell him it's urgent."

"He's dead." Andy's dizzy and only half-listening.

"Oh, I'm sorry to hear that."

"What's so urgent?"

"It's a demon."

Andy bites her lip. "Is it my mom?"

"Yes," answers Christian. "I'm sorry. I didn't know you knew."

"Where is she?"

"Alaska. She's been here for a while. Not sure what she's doing."

"Text me the location. I'll be there as soon as I can."

She sighs. She can't sleep, not while some random person is watching her dead mother. She starts the car and drives until she can't. She pulls over somewhere north of Edmonton. She'd sent Christian a text when she'd crossed into Canada. She'd told him she'd let him know once she reached Alaska.

Andy settles into the back seat of her car to sleep. She just needs to rest her eyes. It's daylight and there are plenty of people coming and going from the area. She pulls her coat over her and tries to sleep. She tries to ignore the voice that says Christian is a stranger and she should have asked more questions. She can't think about that. She can't think about Oriana either. Instead, she's obsessing over the fact that Jeremy must have known the monster had her mother's body. Jeremy knew and didn't tell her. He was prepared when the monster tracked them down, but Andy wasn't.

Jeremy knew.

She wakes up with a crick in her neck half an hour before her alarm goes off. Faith and Ava and Tristan have all called her. She's got messages from them on her phone and Jeremy's. She doesn't know what they say, and she hasn't read any of their texts. Faith still doesn't know the demon is wearing their mother's body. She doesn't know Andy thinks their mother could still be alive. Maybe Ava knows. Maybe Jeremy told her. Maybe when she sees her mother, she'll recognize Andy and she can save her. She shakes her head, trying to banish the thought. She can't get distracted by what-ifs this time. Hope will get her killed.

She grumbles to herself as she pulls back onto the highway.

* * *

Christian is stationed in a small studio apartment in Alaska. The floor is littered with bottles, newspaper clippings, and empty ammo boxes.

Andy arrived earlier in the day.

He is about ten years older than Jeremy, and he was a biologist in another life. He was recruited into the job when an angel tried to possess his daughter. It attacked him and his wife. He killed it but couldn't save his family.

His wife was a teacher and his daughter was very young but showed promise as a musician. After the attack, someone above his pay grade contacted him. Over a bottle of scotch, he tells Andy he's been trapping ever since.

"This life isn't for everybody," says Christian. He downs the rest of his drink and slides the glass to the center of the table.

"Amen to that," says Andy. She finishes her drink and pours two more for them.

"Just about killed your daddy when your kid sister left."

"Yeah, but Faith was made for bigger and better things."

Christian downs his drink in one gulp. "Nothing's bigger and better than saving the world from monsters. We're in the shit every goddamn day so limp-dick little bitches can get up, brush their teeth, drink their coffee and tell themselves they're making a difference."

Andy sips her scotch. He's not wrong, technically, but her mind goes to Oriana. She's not a monster but Andy is. Maybe Christian is a monster too.

Maybe he'll kill Andy and put her out of her misery.

"Mark my words. One day those bastards will come for our world." He pours another glass. "They'll cherry-pick the best and brightest among us to serve them and everybody else is going to be monster chow." He nods to Andy. "People like us make it possible for people like your sister to keep their hands clean."

Andy takes another sip and swallows hard.

"World's full of ingrates."

Andy huffs. "So," she begins, "you said you had a location?"

Christian gestures behind Andy to a roll of paper on the counter.

Andy retrieves it. She stumbles as she crosses the kitchen. She's being stupid. She shouldn't be this drunk around a stranger.

Christian said he's kept a thorough record of the places he's seen the monster. Andy returns to where Christian is sitting and unrolls the map on the table.

"It was a real pain in my ass, tracking her down," says Christian.

Andy looks over the paper. It's covered in red dots where Christian marked sightings of her mother. "I appreciate you keeping tabs on Mom. I owe you one."

Christian's smile fades from his face. He sits up, suddenly serious, and his glossy eyes bore into Andy. "That *thing* is not your mother anymore."

"I know."

"You sure?" He says it like he can see right through her.

"Positive," she lies.

He sits back in his seat. "Make sure you're clear on that before we face it. I'm not going into this fight with a weak link."

She shouldn't drink more, but she does.

Christian is a trapper. If he does kill her, he'll at least know to destroy her body so she won't come back. If whoever is possessing her mother kills her, she won't get a say in what becomes of her body. It doesn't matter. She'll be dead either way. Suddenly, she realizes that's what she wants. She blinks heavily.

"I made up the sofa bed," says Christian. "We can discuss the terms of my service tomorrow."

"Terms of service?"

"Tomorrow."

"Tonight."

"You won't remember anyway," he says. "You're drunk. Sleep it off and we'll talk in the morning."

"If I'm about to make a deal, I deserve to think about it for a night."

Christian examines her again. "Fine. I've got a possession problem of my own."

"Oh?"

He nods. "An angel is on the run, and I told a friend I'd track it down."

"You seem to be fine tracking things on your own."

"It's faster with two people."

"It's half the pay," says Andy. The government compensates per kill and they are encouraged to work alone. When she was seventeen, Andy realized Jeremy trained her and Faith because he'd earn more money for less work.

She didn't blame him, though. The government didn't pay much in trade for their service. Technically their contracts could be terminated at any time. She guessed it was easier to hide evidence of the existence of the program if the need ever came.

"It's a favor," says Christian. "It's not a kill mission. Just track and deliver the intel."

"So, no paycheck?"

"We'll be compensated."

"And you're willing to split the pay with me?"

"Like I said, we'll discuss terms tomorrow."

Andy is too drunk to keep negotiating. "All right. Tomorrow."

CHAPTER FIFTEEN

Oriana waits in the darkness of the Hoh Rainforest, perched high in a giant spruce tree. Since she flew low over several towns along the way, if there are any trappers in the area, they'll know she's close. She's positioned well away from any trails. Anyone who finds her will be someone looking for a monster.

She's been there for several hours. She was careful to leave a trail of feathers and broken branches. She even let tendrils of her power sink into the ground and shake the earth. She can sense a few humans nearby. They could be looking for her. One of them could be her kidnapper.

She hears someone approach. A man with light brown hair steps out of the trees. He's got a gun in his hands. Twigs snap behind Oriana as another human advances. They were wise not to travel alone. The second man is close to the base of the tree and is also armed with a gun. He's got a deep scowl on his face.

Oriana dives.

She knocks the scowling man to the ground and disarms him. She takes a bullet to her wing before she rounds on the second man. She destroys the second gun, but neither trapper is backing down. They're prepared. One of them throws liquid on her back and it burns like fire. The first man draws his knife and lunges. She grabs him by the wrist and tugs until she hears a snap. It would be easier to force them into unconsciousness, but she needs the fight more than the victory. She needs to witness her own strength. She takes the fallen knife and plunges it into the first man's belly, then drops him.

Before the scowling trapper can help his companion, Oriana turns and tackles him to the ground. She stands up and, before he has a chance to crawl away, slams her heel down hard on his thigh. Bones crack and he screams. She's not a fighter but her new strength and justified rage makes it easy to take them down. Blind fury seems to make up for her lack of experience.

Oriana drags the two bleeding men to the base of her tree and props them against the trunk. The first man begins to beg while the other clutches his leg. Oriana pulls a photograph from her pocket. She crouches low and shows the humans the image of a tired face with pale eyes and shaggy blond hair. The man in the picture is happier than Oriana ever saw him in person. He's holding a small girl in his arms and smiling.

She retrieved the photograph from Ava's room, but she assumes Ava got it from the trapper's house. She makes sure both men are paying attention before she growls, "Do you recognize this man?"

The first man whimpers. "Please let us go."

"Do you recognize him?" repeats Oriana, this time louder.

The scowling trapper, still clutching his thigh, spits blood and saliva at Oriana.

"Please," begs the first man. "We've never seen him before." The first man continues to plead.

The scowling man grits his teeth, prepared to die.

Monster.

Oriana stumbles back, wings flaring to steady herself.

Both humans flinch.

Save them, monster.

She stares wide-eyed at the men. She *is* a monster. But maybe instead of running from her wickedness, she can embrace it.

Not everyone is lucky enough to be so warped by torment that they become numb to it.

She watches the first man as he clutches his stomach to stop the bleeding. Oriana feels nothing. For the first time since Faith and Ava found her, she feels nothing again. Nothing can hurt her. Nothing can stop her.

She stands and drags the first man to his feet. She places her palm on his forehead and wills her power to mend the broken places in the human's body. Oriana is clumsy and inexperienced with healing and the man screams, but he survives and the bleeding stops. Color returns to his face and after a minute he grows quiet and gapes at Oriana.

She drops the man back to the ground. "I believe you. Now, run."

Without a second thought for his companion, he disappears into the forest.

Oriana turns to the scowling man who is still glaring at her from the ground. "Do you recognize this man?"

He doesn't answer. He's pale and his breathing is labored. He's still glaring, but his eyes are unfocused. Oriana grabs one of his fingers and snaps it. The man screams. His heartbeat is erratic.

"Answer me!"

"I don't know him!"

"Are you sure?"

"Yes," cries the trapper.

Oriana again lets her power flow into the human. She heals his leg and finger. She steps back, returns the photograph to her pocket, and takes off.

She repeats this process again and again, reaping minor rewards for her efforts. One person recognizes the man in the photo and says he is insane. Another knows him but doesn't share any information until Oriana threatens her husband. Apparently, her kidnapper went north chasing another angel.

She finds another trapper later who confirms her story, though no one knows where he went or how long he's been gone. Frustrated, Oriana corners a man in an alley one night in Seattle.

She slams the human against the cold concrete of the building behind him and growls. She keeps her voice low to avoid calling attention to them. She's got one hand over his mouth and she's so close she can smell the blood dripping from the human's nose.

"It is impossible that no one knows him," says Oriana.

The human is trembling as he struggles to hold himself upright.

"You must know something. Nod your head. Do you know him?"

The human's eyes droop and he doesn't respond. He stops shaking.

"Answer me."

His breathing slows.

Oriana steps back and lets him slump to the ground. She watches as minor convulsions make him twitch. Suddenly a hand clamps down on Oriana's shoulder. Someone shoves her away from the human and she falls. As she stumbles back to her feet, she sees a bright light, hot and powerful. The light silhouettes a figure hovering above the trapper. A glowing hand reaches down and touches his cheek.

The human's eyes snap open and he stares open-mouthed at the figure above him. It pulls him up and then steps aside. He runs.

The light rounds on Oriana. It rushes forward and suddenly they're far away from the city, surrounded by darkness and trees. The light dims and a woman appears. Two massive white wings glimmer behind her in the moonlight. Her eyes glow then that light also fades. When she speaks, her voice is deep and commanding. "It gives me no pleasure to kill one of my own," she says, "but you must be punished."

Oriana's mind is still back in the alley. She's still reeling from the light. "You're an angel," she breathes.

The woman frowns. "Aren't you?"

Oriana almost laughs. As if she can't smell the stain of humanity in her blood. "I'm a mongrel."

She blinks as though Oriana's species makes a difference. A wisp of light uncurls from her hand and disappears around Oriana. "You are human and angel. Why are you attacking humans?"

"Trappers," corrects Oriana. "I'm attacking trappers."

"Can you possess a body?"

Oriana shakes her head.

"Then why are you attacking people?"

"I'm only attacking trappers. I need information on someone."

"Why?"

"He is wicked."

The woman appears unmoved.

"He killed my family—my father."

"Was your father angel or human?"

"Angel."

"You think killing this man will lessen the loss of your father?"

"No," snaps Oriana. "And I never said I intend to kill him." She feels a sting in the center of her chest.

"It seems fair to draw that conclusion."

Oriana sighs. "Are you going to kill me or can I go?"

"I haven't decided yet. What is your name?"

Her chest stings again. "Oriana."

"My name is Ariel. I am the guardian of this region." She examines her, still scowling. "I will keep you."

Oriana flinches away from her. "No, I will not be owned again."

Ariel makes a motion with her hand. "Elaborate."

Oriana clutches a hand to her chest. Ariel is compelling her to speak using her power. Can Oriana do that? Can she counter the effect? She stares back at her and concentrates on the feeling in her chest. After a minute, something snaps and it's easier to breathe.

Ariel tilts her head to one side. "So, you *can* fight back. Interesting."

Once again Oriana finds herself negotiating the terms of her release. The terms are always the same. "Either kill me or let me go."

Ariel nods. "Eventually, I will do one or the other. But I will keep you until I've made my decision."

Oriana flares her wings. "No."

"Do not challenge me. You will lose."

She could flee. She's fast, much faster than she was even as a child. She stands her ground. She will *not* run. She *will* fight and maybe die, and then maybe this will all be over.

Ariel plants her feet, ready to meet her charge. Oriana knows better than to attack first, but her blood is surging hot through her veins, and she will not be held captive again. She lunges. Ariel grabs her shoulder, flicks her wrist, something snaps and Oriana collapses onto her stomach. Ariel touches her arm and heals the break, then plants her foot in the center of Oriana's back to keep her from standing again. "Surely you didn't think that would work?"

Oriana struggles, but she has her pinned.

"Use an aura," she says.

"What?"

"Aura."

"I heard you," she says, grunting under the weight of Ariel's foot. "I don't know what that is."

"It's your power. Humans call it magic."

Oriana's father never called it that.

"No?" asks Ariel. "I win? Just like that?" She laughs. "A real angel would not surrender so quickly. What would your father think?"

Oriana growls and places both hands beneath her and attempts to push herself up.

"Aura," she says.

"Is this a game to you?" she grunts.

"No. It is as painful for me as it is humiliating for you." Ariel presses her foot harder into her back. "Take my advice or die in the dirt like your human ancestors." She pauses and Oriana can almost hear the taunt before she says it. "Die in the dirt, as I'm sure your mother did when she gave birth to you."

That's the tipping point. She pushes against the ground, power curling between muscles to boost her strength. She throws the angel off and charges as she tumbles back. She grabs her shoulders and holds her against a tree. "How do you know about my mother?"

Ariel sighs. Her expression is not one of shock or fear—it's pity. "Humans rarely survive the birth of a hybrid."

Oriana releases her. "What?"

"And most hybrids do not live as long as you have."

Her body chills and the change in energy is too much.

Ariel takes a step forward. "Did you think you were the only one?"

"Hybrids," repeats Oriana.

"That's what you are."

Monster. Mongrel. Abomination.

"There are others?" she asks.

"A few. Would you like to meet one?"

Oriana doesn't answer.

Ariel steps closer and takes her hand. "Come with me." It's an invitation, not a command. She takes her to a house on the edge of an island somewhere Oriana doesn't recognize. The living room window looks out over the sea. She leads her into the house, still holding her hand. Ariel travels in bursts of light powered by her auras.

Oriana's not sure it really counts as flying.

"The hybrid you are going to meet is still a child," says Ariel. "Her name is Dina. Angels killed her parents because her creation was an act of treason. Her mother was an angel and her father was human."

Oriana is still too stunned to speak, so Ariel continues, "Heather was Dina's mother. I don't know if you knew her, but Heather knew Carolus."

Oriana starts at the name, her father's name. A name she hasn't heard or dared to speak in decades. Ariel must sense her discomfort, because she extends her power through their linked hands and Oriana feels, rather than hears, her apology.

"Sit," she says, releasing her hand. She nudges her toward a piece of overstuffed furniture that vaguely resembles a chair with no back.

The seat is comfortable and high enough that Oriana's wings do not touch the floor when she sits. She hears voices in the back of the house.

Carolus.

Her kidnapper never knew her father's name. It was the only thing he was unable to take. Oriana gave up her own name after only a few days alone, but she never gave up Carolus.

Ariel said it so casually. Did she know him?

A male voice gets Oriana's attention. She's not alone anymore. A man, another angel with large white wings, stands in front of her, grinning. "Cool," he says. "Black wings." He extends his hand to Oriana. "I'm Josiah—"

"I told you to wait," Ariel says.

"And then you said she was a hybrid. I'm going to get Tabbris."

"No!" shouts Ariel, but Josiah has already disappeared. "Damn it."

Josiah reappears just as suddenly, this time accompanied by a man and a woman. "This is the new angel. New angel, this is Tabbris and Lailah." He gestures to the man and the woman respectively.

"Her name is Oriana," says Ariel.

"Can she hide her wings?" asks Tabbris.

"Can you hide your wings?" asks Lailah.

Oriana shakes her head.

There is a flash of light, and the two newcomers manifest their wings. They are also white.

Tabbris nudges Ariel. "And you say we don't have manners."

"I've never seen black wings before," says Lailah.

"They're weird, right?" asks Josiah. "I mean cool-weird, but still—weird." Something resembling a small bolt of lightning strikes Josiah from the side. He jumps and clutches at the scorch mark.

"I warned you," says Ariel.

"Excessive," snaps Josiah. "I clarified 'cool-weird.'"

Tabbris and Lailah snicker, but the room quiets when a small voice calls out, "Ariel?"

A child emerges from the hall and immediately seeks refuge behind Ariel.

Oriana stands. It's too much. This is not reality. She can't be with other angels. There isn't someone else like her. She's been captured again, or maybe she's dying, still in the darkness of the alleyway. This is an illusion. This is not her world.

Oriana tries to back away, but the ridiculous chair is blocking her. She does a bumbling sort of sidestep with no real destination in mind. Beyond the chair is the wall. Beyond the wall is a world in which she is not welcome. But this isn't real—it can't be—it's a dream, and she cannot run from a dream.

"Take it easy, Oriana," says Josiah.

"I told you," says Ariel.

"You also said she's an adult. I didn't think she'd scare so easily."

"You three are enough to scare anyone," says Ariel.

Oriana closes her eyes. Her world is dark and bloody and lonesome. She almost had a family, but she left them. She misses them. She misses Ava and Faith and Tristan and Andy.

Hands close over hers. She didn't realize her hands were clenched into fists until strong, but gentle fingers intertwine with hers.

"Oriana?" asks Ariel.

Dreams can speak. They can speak, shout, sing, hurt, break, anything she can imagine; her dreams can make it seem real.

Andy.

She tries to conjure her. She imagines Andy apologizing and cupping her cheek.

Something tugs at one of her flight feathers and she quickly opens her eyes.

The child, presumably Dina, steps away from her, hands clutched to her chest and head ducked in apology. Her wings are charcoal gray, but Oriana can detect shadows of blue in the light. She's small, too small to be alone and younger than Oriana was when she was alone.

"Sorry," she whispers. She retreats to Ariel's side.

Oriana looks from the girl to the other angels. "This does not feel real," she says.

"I know," says Ariel. "It will be a difficult adjustment, but you will become accustomed to it soon."

"I don't want to stay."

"Nobody's forcing you," says Josiah.

Ariel bites her lip. "I sort of threatened her to get her to come here."

"Of course you did," mutters Josiah.

"You don't have to stay," says Ariel, voice softer than it has been. "I just wanted you to see us and meet Dina."

Oriana nods.

"You'll have to stop attacking the people in my territory, though," adds Ariel.

She nods again.

Ariel releases her hands and steps back, ushering Dina along with her. "It was nice to meet you," she says.

"Nice to meet you," echoes Dina quietly.

Oriana inches toward the door and no one moves to stop her.

"Bye, I guess," says Josiah, sounding somewhat reluctant.

Tabbris and Lailah wave.

"Sorry about the wings thing," says Lailah. "Nice meeting you."

"Yeah," says Tabbris. "Ditto."

Oriana moves to the door without turning her back to them. Josiah was right, no one is forcing her to stay.

"You know you don't have to leave straight away, right?" asks Ariel. "You are welcome to stay the night."

Is that a trap? Perhaps she's found the caveat. They force her here, let her think she has a choice, then when she stays, she's imprisoned and it's by her own free will. That seems like the right level of twisted for her reality. Perhaps this isn't a dream.

Her hand lands on the doorknob. It's not locked. She opens the door and backs outside into the night. She shuts the door

and keeps backing away. Maybe they want to chase her. Maybe
that's the caveat. She puts as much distance between her and the
house as she can without flying.

The front yard drops off in a steep decline that ends in the
sea. Waves lap at the rocks below her. She waits for one of the
angels to leave, waits for the chase to begin. They can probably
sense her still standing there.

Nothing happens. She can hear voices inside the house. She
sees figures move through the curtains covering the windows.
She belongs outside, separated from the warm light of the
house. She belongs alone. She knows how to be alone. She can't
form a bond with people, knowing one day it will break due to
cruelty or inevitability. She can't lose another family. She's not
strong enough, but she wants to be.

CHAPTER SIXTEEN

Andy wakes up to the sound of Christian rummaging around in the kitchen. She groans as she sits up and holds her head in her hands. She has a throbbing headache and her mouth is too dry. She looks to the kitchen. Christian isn't paying any attention to her. He's busy with the coffeepot.

She slowly pushes herself up and wobbles to steady herself against the back of a chair.

"Morning," says Christian.

"Morning."

He didn't kill her in her sleep, but that doesn't mean she can trust him yet.

"How much of last night do you remember?" he asks.

"Enough." That's true for the most part. They had a deal. Fuck. Did they make a deal while she was drunk? What did she agree to?

He opens the refrigerator and pulls out orange juice, eggs, and tabasco. He cracks an egg into a glass followed by a healthy amount of hot sauce. He fills the glass the rest of the way with orange juice. He sets the drink on the counter. "Drink up."

Andy makes a face. Trappers are notorious for their hangover cures. She drinks the concoction nonetheless.

"So, about our arrangement."

Right. Christian needs help finding something, too. Andy vaguely remembers discussing it. "Yeah?" she asks.

"I'll help you find your demon if you help me find my angel."

"Yeah, I'll help you. Remind me why you need help?"

"I'll give you the details after we catch the thing that killed your mom."

"I'm not going into a deal blind."

"I'll let you keep the money for the first kill."

"For the demon? You'll let me keep the entire paycheck?"

He nods.

"Why?"

"I need help."

"I want the paycheck from both kills," says Andy.

"We're not killing mine."

"Then we don't get paid."

"I know."

"So why would I agree to help you?"

"Because you can't kill your demon alone."

"Says who?" Andy huffs.

"Says me, and your dead daddy."

She frowns.

"He told me you have a soft spot when it comes to your mom."

How did Jeremy know that? Was Andy that easy to read?

"If you hesitate at all, that monster will kill you," continues Christian. "You need me."

Andy raises an eyebrow. "Are you doing me a favor so I'll be indebted to you?"

"Yep."

"What makes you think I'll hold up my end of the deal?"

"You're Jeremy's daughter."

She folds her arms. "So?"

"So, I know you'll repay your debt."

"Maybe I don't need you. Maybe I can do this alone."

"You can't, but if you want to try, I'm not going to stop you."

Andy doesn't need help. She doesn't really want help, either. She doesn't like being forced into owing someone but at least Christian is honest about it. She has the information she needed. He's pointed her in the right direction. She can figure it out on her own from here.

"You'd really rather fight that thing alone than owe me a favor?" he presses.

Andy shrugs. "I don't like owing people."

Christian takes a sip of his coffee.

Andy examines him. "I think," she says slowly, "you need me more than I need you."

He laughs. "Honey, I don't *need* you at all."

"Then I guess we're done here. Thanks for letting me crash on your couch."

"I know about your sister."

"What's that supposed to mean?"

"I know that she works with Ava and I know what they do."

Andy plays dumb. "Oh really? What do they do?"

"They're traitors. Ava feeds false information to people like me who are out here trying to save the damn world from monsters."

"What exactly are you saying?"

"I'm saying you can help me, or I can tell a very interested group of very dangerous people the truth about your family."

"You're going to blackmail me into helping you?"

"If that's what it takes, yes."

Andy literally bites her tongue to keep from saying something that would make her situation worse.

"You're a smart girl. You know what would happen to them, what the community would do, and you know the government would turn a blind eye. Technically what they're doing is illegal."

Andy doesn't say anything. Now Christian is a fucking problem, and he must be dealt with. She nods slowly, more to herself than to him. She needs to confirm her suspicions. "How do you know what Ava does?"

"Jeremy."

"So, if I help you, you'll leave my family out of this?"

He nods.

"How do I know I can trust you to keep your word?"

"I'll trade you a secret for a secret."

"Okay, what's your secret?"

He clicks his tongue. "Not yet."

"I told you, I'm not going into this blind."

"You don't get to call the shots here."

Andy licks her lips. She's got a plan forming. She'll play along while they work. She can't let him leave her sight in case he decides to go rogue. She doesn't know his skill set but he must be pretty good to have survived this long alone. Apparently, he knew Jeremy. He probably knows others. Would he be missed if he went missing? Who would come looking for him?

She needs to answer those questions before she deals with him. She'll let him help find her mom, then fuck up the attack enough to let him get killed. She let Jeremy get killed. She's murdered plenty of angels and demons. It's not like there isn't blood on her hands already.

One more kill in the name of saving her family won't mean much in the grand scheme of morality. Hell, she might just shoot him in the head once they get somewhere more secluded. One thing she knows for certain is that she's not letting him get away.

"Do we have a deal?" asks Christian.

She nods. "Yeah. Deal."

"Good. Get your shit. We've got a lead on the demon."

"My shit is in my car."

"Get it. I'm driving."

"No, we'll take separate cars."

"Nope. I'm not letting you out of my sight that long. Don't want you warning Ava."

"I won't warn her. You have my word."

"Yeah, see, that's the thing. Your word isn't any good now that I've threatened you."

"So, what? I'm a hostage?"

"Don't be dramatic. We're partners. I scratch your back, you scratch mine. I just don't trust you not to do something stupid in the meantime."

Andy rubs her forehead. She wasn't planning on calling Ava anyway, but if Christian is already suspicious, it's going to make killing him a lot harder.

They pack what they need for the search and head into Alaska. They take Christian's SUV. It's loaded with weapons, food, water, and tire chains should the roads get icy. Christian drives.

She saw it as soon as she got into the vehicle. A small, single black feather dangles on a leather band from the rearview mirror. It glitters with soft hues of purple and green when the sunlight catches it.

Christian sees her staring. "Ever seen black wings before?"

Andy swallows the lump in her throat. "No."

"My angel has black wings."

"That should make it easy to identify."

He nods. "They make a damn fine trophy, too."

"Do I get the trophy, or do you?" asks Andy casually.

"I do. But I'll let you keep some feathers."

"I thought we weren't trying to kill your angel."

"You don't have to kill an angel to take their wings."

She swallows her anger. "Right. I didn't think about that."

Christian doesn't know it, but as far as Andy's concerned, he's sealed his fate. He has to die. She just needs to decide how she's going to do it.

"So," he says, "got any good war stories? We've got some time to kill before we reach the spot of the last sighting."

They have fourteen hours, to be exact.

"I've got a lot of war stories, but I don't know if any of them are good. How about you?"

She doesn't want to talk. There was a time when she'd sit and drink and go on about her latest and greatest kill. But now it makes her sick.

"I've got some, but I'd rather hear from you. I'm driving. It's your job to keep me awake."

"All right. I'll trade you a story for a story."

"Sounds fair."

Andy starts telling him about a case she worked with Jeremy. It was a tough one because the demon had possessed a child. Andy doused the poor kid in holy water and Jeremy finished it off. She swallows hard. There's no glory in her stories anymore. She's just a murderer.

They keep talking until they reach their destination. It's fourteen hours of Andy confessing her sins and hating herself with every word. They pull into the parking lot of the only hotel around. It's cold and it's obvious this isn't a tourist town. The hotel is an oasis in the middle of an arctic desert.

Andy offers to take their overnight bags to the room while Christian looks into a flight to Utqiagvik.

"No," he says. "Stay with me. I can't let you wander off."

They book a flight. They have a long trip to Utqiagvik. From there, Christian has secured snowmobiles and another hotel room. They don't have a return flight since there's no way to know how long this will take.

After all the talking they did, Andy expects Christian to keep the conversation going, but he doesn't. He gets quiet over dinner and keeps to himself. Instead of going to bed, he hunches over a notebook. He uses a single black feather as a bookmark. It makes Andy's blood boil, but she doesn't say anything about it.

CHAPTER SEVENTEEN

Oriana approaches the door to the angels' house. Since she was allowed to return to Ava's after choosing to leave, maybe she is allowed to return here as well. Maybe leaving isn't permanent. Maybe returning isn't permanent either. Maybe this is freedom.

She's been standing outside staring at the house for an hour. She knocks. She knows they are still gathered in the living room. The house quiets as soon as her knuckles meet wood.

It's Josiah who swings the door open and invites her back inside. "Miss us already?"

"Yes."

"Really?"

"Yes."

It must have been a joke. Andy had similarly surprised reactions when Oriana responded to sarcasm with honesty. She glances around the room and stops at Dina, who's sitting beside Ariel, wiping tears away from her eyes.

"Welcome back," says Ariel.

Tabbris hands her a drink.

"She's going to need something stronger than that," says Lailah.

"That's 150 proof," says Tabbris, pointing to the drink.

"Mix it with this," Lailah says, handing Oriana another bottle.

Josiah intervenes and takes the bottle instead, then turns to Oriana. "If you learn nothing else while you're here, know that you should never, ever, take drink advice from these two."

Oriana is still watching Dina. "Is she hurt?"

Her chubby cheeks are bright pink and she fidgets with the hem of her dress.

"She's never met another hybrid," answers Ariel. "She's glad you're back."

Dina clutches the sleeve of Ariel's shirt and mutters something. Oriana is suddenly very aware of her tattered appearance. She's been fighting and hasn't had the chance to look more presentable. She shifts her wings, immediately embarrassed. She's in a room full of angels and the movement does not go unnoticed.

"Sorry," says Josiah. "Sometimes I'm actually as rude as Ariel claims. Do you want to change clothes? You can borrow some of ours."

Oriana is still focused on the child.

"Come on," continues Josiah. "I'll show you around the house and get you changed. Are you hungry?"

Oriana is starving and her stomach growls.

Josiah laughs. "Or we can do food first." He motions for her to follow him into the kitchen. "Food is so much better in this dimension, but our booze is the best. Pair that with some pizza and I'm in paradise." He pulls out a chair, then goes to the refrigerator.

Oriana notices all the furniture in the house is elevated to accommodate the length of wings when someone sits down.

"Speaking of which, we've got leftover pizza. You want some?"

"Yes, please." She's still looking back toward the living room. The others seem to be giving her space.

"You want to go back in there?"

"Not particularly."

"Okay, just checking. Ariel said if you came back in the house we had to behave better and not crowd you."

"You knew I was waiting outside?"

"Yeah, but I was pretty sure you were going to leave. Glad I didn't put any money on that."

Oriana smiles. Andy's used a similar expression. It's a reference to gambling, and she understands it.

He has a plate with a few slices of pizza on it. "Do you want me to heat this up?"

"No thank you." She had pizza one night with Faith, Tristan, and Ava. She's familiar with the dish and it's another thing she doesn't have to ask about.

"Suit yourself," he says, passing her the plate.

She eats quickly and he reheats the rest of the pizza because he says she'll want more later, and he can't, in good conscious, let her keep eating it cold. He does this despite her insistence that she's full.

Once she's finished her meal, Josiah shows her around the house. The ceilings are high, the doorways are wide, and rooms are spacious. Everything is designed just on the cusp of inconspicuous so if a human stopped by, it could pass for unique instead of "specifically tailored for angels."

Josiah explains that there are four bedrooms in total—one for Dina, Ariel, Josiah, and then the spare room. They are currently in Ariel's room searching for clothing.

"Where do Tabbris and Lailah stay?" asks Oriana.

"They don't live with us. Their turf is in the UK."

"UK?"

"United Kingdom."

Oriana has learned enough basic geography to understand the UK is very far away from their current location. She assumes they are still somewhere in or near the Pacific Northwest since Ariel said Seattle was part of her territory. That leads her to another question. "Why do you have different territories? Do all angels have territory?"

Josiah shakes his head. "Nah, we're kind of self-appointed guardians of certain places around the world. It doesn't always work out so well, though. Ariel was stationed on the east coast about four hundred years ago. They saw her use her grace and thought she was a witch. Bunch of assholes tried to kill her."

"Four hundred years ago?" She's a baby by comparison. "You must have seen so much history."

Josiah shrugs. "I guess. We go back and forth from this world to home. Turns out, dimension hopping wreaks havoc on your age." He finishes pawing through the closet, then tosses an armful of clothes to Oriana. "Bathroom is right across from your room. Technically we've got two bathrooms, but Ariel and Dina have claimed the other one and the flower smell is so strong it's like someone's beating you to death with a garden."

He makes a face. "Dina is going through this candle collecting phase and it's just impossible to say no to her when she wants something. You can share my bathroom. Towels and soap and stuff are on the shelf."

"Thank you."

"You're welcome. And one more thing, if you don't feel like coming back out to hang with us, don't worry about it. I don't know what your story is, but clearly, you've seen some shit. If you want to just relax in your room, raid the kitchen, or take a walk or flight or whatever, that's fine. You're a guest. You can do what you want."

Oriana cocks her head to the side, eyebrow raised. "Did Ariel tell you to say that?"

Josiah rubs the back of his neck. "Kinda. We're also not supposed to pressure you to talk, and we need to respect your boundaries. Don't get me wrong," he hurries to clarify, "we'd do that stuff anyway. Ariel's just the nicest one around here so we defer to her judgment."

"You all seem very nice to me."

"We're not so bad once you get to know us."

He leaves and Oriana goes into the bathroom. She scrubs herself clean. She does what she can to rid her wings of dirt and human blood, but she can't quite reach some of the feathers.

After a while, she stops trying and just lets the warm water pound against her back. She leans her forehead against the tile and closes her eyes. The water pressure is comforting, almost like fingers running through her feathers.

She rests a hand over her heart. She suddenly feels lonely.

After her shower, she gets dressed. She struggles with the shirt, but eventually figures it out. It's similar to the shirts she wore at Ava's, with buttons at the back for her wings.

When she returns to the living room Ariel gives her an encouraging smile and invites her to sit with her and Dina on the couch. Dina watches her every move, and as Oriana sits beside her, Dina twists to face her. It takes her a while to say something. "Were your wings always black?" she asks.

"Yes."

She looks confused.

"Our wings are unique. That's a good thing."

Dina nods. "Do your wings go away?"

"No." Oriana notices the room is quiet. The others are listening.

"Mine don't go away either," she says. "Have you met any humans?"

"Yes."

Dina gasps. "What are they like? Are they nice or are they bad?"

"They are all different. They have different personalities, just like angels."

"How old are you?"

"I'm not sure. I feel old."

"I'm five." She holds up her fingers to illustrate the point. "When is your birthday?"

"August first."

Her line of questioning continues until she starts to yawn midconversation.

Ariel pets her hair. "Bedtime."

"No," says Dina. "I'm not sleepy."

"I am," says Oriana.

"Me too," says Josiah. He shoots Tabbris and Lailah a look and they agree.

"We'll all go to sleep," says Ariel. "That way you won't miss anything."

Dina crosses her arms. "You're just going to send me to bed and keep talking."

"We won't," says Oriana.

Dina sighs. "No, it's okay." She slides off the couch and takes Ariel's hand. "I don't want to sleep late and miss anything in the morning." She sighs again. "It's nice to meet you, Oriana. I'm very glad you came back."

"Me too."

Seemingly satisfied, she bids the room good night and leaves with Ariel in tow.

"Precocious little thing," mutters Lailah.

"You should hear her when she gets mad," says Josiah. "She'll make a hell of a guardian one day."

"She'll be a guardian?" asks Oriana.

"That's what she says she wants to do."

"Could I be a guardian?" Oriana asks.

"Sure," answers Josiah. "Ariel will have to approve you, but we can teach you and assign you a territory if that's what you want."

Oriana tries not to let herself get excited. She curls her wings around her shoulders. She'd be in charge of protecting humans. She needs to prove she can defend instead of destroy.

"Why does that upset you?" asks Lailah gently.

"I'm not upset," answers Oriana.

"You look upset," says Tabbris.

"You don't have to be a guardian," says Josiah.

Ariel returns. She examines Oriana for a moment, then sits beside her and extends a large white wing behind her. "Did they give you any trouble while I was gone?"

"No."

"She asked about being a guardian," says Tabbris.

"I can teach you to be a guardian," says Ariel. "If that's what you want."

"Thank you."

She knows they're waiting for her to say more. She doesn't mean to abandon the conversation. At some point they will want to know about her past. They trust her enough to let her stay. They trust her to be around a child. Ariel knows what she's capable of, the destruction she leaves in her wake. But she doesn't know everything. They deserve to know.

She bites her lip and stares at the floor. "Before you decide to let me stay in your house," she begins, "it's only fair that you know my history."

Ariel pulls her closer with her wing and rests a hand on her knee. "You don't owe us an explanation."

"I'd like to tell you now." *Before it's too late. Before you find out and change your mind.*

The angels don't stop her.

Tabbris pours another drink and passes it to Oriana. She swallows the contents in one gulp and Tabbris hands her the bottle. She takes another drink before she starts talking. Whatever Tabbris gave her is more potent than Andy's liquor. She starts with her mother. She does her best to explain her father's wrath against humans. He was only trying to defend his daughter.

She takes another drink when she introduces the trapper. She keeps it brief and struggles to find a way to explain the many, many lives she could have saved had she not been so selfish. Her entire life is summed up in just a few sentences. At some point, Ariel takes her hand. The hollow feeling spreads through her chest again.

When she begins to explain her escape, she leaves Andy out of the story. She's not sure why. In this version no one sings her through her nightmares. No one lets her pretend to fly. No one helps her burn away her past. No one teaches her to be human. Her time at Ava's is much easier to explain without Andy. She ends her story by telling them she healed enough to find the trapper. The kind humans helped her recover and let her leave when she was ready. That's it.

The angels wait a moment to make sure she's done with her story. Their silence encourages her.

"I didn't share my story with you to elicit sympathy. I wanted you all to know I may not be mentally stable enough to watch over a territory or even stay in your home."

"You are not the first abused person to stay in this house," says Ariel. "I hope you don't feel like you have to confess to us."

"But it's nice that you're honest," adds Lailah.

"We should probably be honest, too," says Josiah. "We're guardians now, but we all began as warriors and, yikes, I've killed a shitload of people." He smiles and for the first time it doesn't look like he's happy about it.

"Same here," says Tabbris. "Though, I'd wager Lailah's killed more than both of us combined."

"Demons don't count," says Lailah.

Tabbris laughs. "Spoken like a stone-cold killer."

"Point being," says Ariel, "you're in good company. We're all a little fucked-up and more than a little damaged. I've got a feeling you'll fit in with us just fine."

Oriana relaxes her wings a little. Every time she tells her story, her memories sting a little less and it's a little easier for her to believe she could belong.

CHAPTER EIGHTEEN

Oriana draws blood with the first punch. Her knuckles split and she hears Josiah's nose crack. She backs away and unclenches her fists. "I'm sorry."

They're training, helping Oriana get stronger.

Oriana looks to her knuckles, wills her aura to the spot, and watches the skin mend before her eyes. She's always healed quickly, but her aura makes the process ever faster.

Ariel approaches them. "Josiah is stronger than you. He will use that to his advantage. You must fight smart. Auras are your advantage against humans. Wit will have to be your advantage against enochs."

Oriana frowns at the term. "Enochs?"

"Angels and demons," answers Ariel. She checks to make sure Oriana has healed correctly. "You used your aura to speed the process. Good." She returns to the sidelines where Dina is waiting. "Again."

Josiah erupts in a ball of blinding light, then appears not even a yard away from Oriana. He strikes hard, then kicks one leg out from under her so she falls.

"Boo!" shouts Dina. "That's cheating."

Josiah doesn't break concentration to retort back. Oriana hurries to her feet, but Josiah strikes her, not with his hand, maybe with an aura. It happened too quickly. Oriana charges back and Josiah stumbles. She shoots into the sky and prepares to dive, but she doesn't have time to heal. She doesn't need it. She shuts out the pain and then plummets back to the ground.

Josiah sees her coming, predicts her next move and retreats. Oriana has just enough time to tuck her wings as she hurtles to the ground. She braces for impact, but it doesn't come. She's still airborne.

Ariel caught her.

"Nice try," she says. She sets Oriana back on the ground.

"But?"

"But Josiah is faster than you. You played into one of his strengths. Find a weakness."

Oriana sighs. "I'm not sure I understand why I am being trained to fight ang—enochs. I do not intend to harm them."

"Then it will be really easy for them to kill you," says Josiah.

Ariel hushes him and her eyes dart to Dina. "Your creation was forbidden," she whispers, one hand on her arm. "There are some who would kill you for the perceived sins of your parents." Dina doesn't seem to hear them and it seems that's on purpose. "If you are going to become a guardian, you will need to be able to protect yourself as well as your charges."

"We should probably start her out against Tabbris," says Josiah. "Then Lailah, then me, then you."

Oriana is confused. "But Tabbris is bigger than all of you. Is he not the strongest?"

Josiah laughs. "Hell no. Tabbris's human form is tall, and generally speaking, the guy is pretty strong, but he was never big on fighting."

"You don't need to pit me against your weakest. I am perfectly capable of training against you."

"It's not a slight against you," says Josiah. "We're just stronger. Think of him as level one. You'll get some wins in, find his weakness, hone your skills and get an ego boost along the way." He leans closer to Oriana and away from Ariel. "Ego is half the battle."

Ariel rolls her eyes. "Overconfidence is intimidating, but only until your opponent recognizes your bravado for what it is."

Oriana tries to hide her smile. Ariel is a good teacher.

They spar for the rest of the afternoon. Oriana lands several effective hits, but Josiah still wins every match. Tabbris and Lailah have business to tend to in their territory. They will not return until tomorrow.

In the evening, Josiah makes dinner while Oriana sits with Ariel. Dina runs back and forth from the living room to the kitchen. Apparently, she is helping with dinner. When Dina leaves the room again, Oriana lowers her voice. She is finally ready to ask a question that's been burning in her since she arrived.

"How did you know my father?" she asks.

"We fought together," answers Ariel.

"How did you know I was his daughter? I never told you."

"I heard he had a daughter with black wings."

Oriana braces herself for the next question. "Was he a guardian?"

Ariel's hesitation gives her answer away. "No."

"This place was not his territory?"

"No. This area was unguarded for close to one hundred years before we arrived."

Oriana's disappointment must show in her face because Ariel continues, "The fighting in our world escalated about a century ago. It was the deadliest period I can remember. Most guardians, like me and Josiah, returned home to help fight."

Oriana waits. Did her father fight? Did he run? Did he kill?

"Carolus fought with us until the enoch exodus into this world. He was stationed here to find and destroy as many people as he could." A frown ghosts across her face. "I think, at some point, the killing became too much. He stopped fighting. We lost contact with him after that. After years of silence, we counted him among the fallen." She hangs her head. "I had no idea he needed help."

Oriana knows she should offer her comfort, but the words stick in her throat.

"I could have helped him," says Ariel. "I thought he was a coward. I never tried to find him." Her wings shift behind her. "I could have helped you, too. I became guardian of this area almost ten years ago. I'm so sorry I didn't find you sooner."

"That's not your fault."

Ariel sighs and looks up at Oriana. "You remind me so much of him."

"Of—of my father?"

"Yes. It's your aura. I knew you were his daughter as soon as I felt it." She gives her a faint smile. "And your wings."

Oriana doesn't get to respond. They both turn toward the sound of little feet rushing into the room.

Dina stops in front of them and takes a moment to catch her breath. "Dinner is ready."

"Thank you," says Oriana.

Dina holds out a hand and Oriana realizes she intends to escort her to the dining room. "Oh, thank you."

"You are the guest of honor," she says. She leads her to the head of the table, then takes a seat beside her while Ariel helps Josiah bring out plates and dishes.

Dina chatters away through most of the meal. She offers Oriana fighting advice. "Just keep hitting Josiah in the face." And she begs to let tomorrow be about aura training so she can participate as well.

Ariel makes no promises, but Oriana suspects Dina will get her way.

Oriana goes to bed early, exhausted by the day and eager for tomorrow's training.

She wakes up breathing in dust. She's lying facedown in the dirt. She coughs and rolls over onto her side.

Josiah is near her. Was he always there?

"We can't find Dina," he says.

Ava runs a hand through her hair and scowls.

They are suddenly in the living room. They are not alone, but Oriana can't make out the faces of the other people. Andy is not among them.

"The trapper took her," says Josiah.

"Andy wouldn't take her without telling us," says Ava.

"You don't know what she would do," says Josiah.

Oriana can still hear them, but she's not in the room with them anymore. She's walking back outside. She drifts away from the house and into the woods. She doesn't drift for long, but she knows the house is far away. She's alone.

Oriana's wings snap shut. They're pressed tight against her back.

The trapper appears and stalks closer.

Oriana's arms are weak at her sides. Her chest is heavy with a throbbing pain. Her knees buckle and she falls.

The trapper emerges and kneels beside Oriana, who reaches out to her.

The trapper takes her hand, entwining their fingers. "You should have stayed at the house, Ana," she says.

"Why did you leave?" She's too weak to sit up straight. She's in the dirt again.

Andy runs her fingers through Oriana's hair and hushes her. "It's okay. You don't understand."

A wave of heat washes over Oriana. Her muscles stretch and swell. She sits up and reaches out to Andy again. Instead of touching her, a white light bursts from her face.

Oriana gasps as her consciousness floods back from the dream. The light is on in her room. She sits up, clutching her chest. Ariel is standing at the foot of her bed, brow furrowed.

"Who is Andy?" she asks.

"Who?"

"You were talking in your sleep. Who is Andy?"

"A human."

"Why haven't you mentioned this human before?"

"It's complicated."

"Elaborate."

Oriana waves her hand before Ariel has a chance to compel her with an aura. "She's a trapper."

"The one who—"

"No. She was a friend."

"Was?"

Oriana sighs. "It's not important. I'm sorry I woke you."

"It is important to me," says Ariel. "You took great care to tell us your story. The fact that you omitted this human is significant."

"It's personal."

"Everything you've told us is personal."

"Ariel, please."

She folds her arms. "Tell me."

Oriana's feathers ruffle. "We were romantically involved. It did not last long. She was—is—the doctor's sister. We had a fight and left the house at the same time. That's it."

"Where is she now?"

"I don't know."

"She is the reason you left."

"Yes."

"Then you lied."

"No," says Oriana quickly. "Well, partially. I was angry when I left, but I left with the intention of finding my captor."

"Why did Andy leave?"

"I don't know. She was angry as well."

"You were romantically involved with a *trapper*, and you left her after a fight?"

"She left first, but yes that's it in summary."

Ariel scowls at her. "A *trapper*."

"Yes—well, not anymore—I'm not sure. She was very conflicted. She has a lot of shame about her past."

"We will need the full story. If she comes looking for you, she might find Dina. She is not ready to meet a human, much less a trapper."

"She won't look for me."

"You separated after an unresolved fight, correct?"

"Yes."

"She has no means to contact you, correct?"

"Correct," answers Oriana.

"There is a strong chance she will search for you."

"Why are you more worried about Andy searching for me than you are about the other trapper searching for me?" asks Oriana. "Andy isn't cruel. She isn't dangerous."

"She is your weakness. That means she is also our weakness." She gestures to the door. "Come. We need to tell the others."

CHAPTER NINETEEN

Andy and Christian land in Utqiagvik late at night. They go to their hotel room and crash. Christian still doesn't say much. Apparently, he only needed to talk long enough to threaten Andy.

The demon is close. Angels and demons are hard to kill if you don't know their weaknesses. Andy knows how to lure and wound, apparently so does Christian.

Children are going missing. They're easy targets for the demon to feed off and drain their lifeforce. The town is blaming a disease, but Christian has mapped out a pattern across Alaska and there's always a sighting of a woman matching Andy's mother's description. Jeremy probably had a network of people keeping an eye out for her, and it seems she's more active than she's been in the past. Killing Jeremy was probably freeing for her. The demon doesn't have to be so careful.

The person who rented them the snowmobiles confirmed another sighting. The demon could vanish anytime. The fact that she's sticking around does not bode well. She probably knows she's being followed. She knows Andy and she got a good look at her the last time they met. She might know Christian too. She's probably eager to kill the people who've been following her for the past few decades. Andy knows the only reason the demon is somewhere remote is to lure her somewhere without backup.

It's dark out. The sun won't rise again for another few months. Someone saw a woman wandering across the tundra south of them. When the witness tried to approach her, she vanished.

Andy cranks up her snowmobile. The witness agrees to lead them to the spot where they saw the woman. They ride single file through the snow with Andy in the middle.

The witness waits with them for about an hour, but then the wind picks up. They warn Andy and Christian not to stay out too long before leaving them to search for the demon alone.

Christian doesn't say a damn word while they wait. Andy paces to stay warm. Another hour passes. They take turns walking out into the snow to check the horizon for anything unusual. When Andy returns from her scouting shift, Christian is straddling his snowmobile.

Andy's weapons are scattered in the snow. Her supply bag is strapped to the back of Christian's vehicle. He cranks his snowmobile to life as Andy approaches.

"Oriana," shouts Christian.

Andy freezes to the spot.

"You thought I didn't know?" shouts Christian. He's already got a gun in his hand.

"I don't know what you're talking about!"

"Don't play dumb with me." He aims behind her and fires a shot into the engine of her snowmobile. "Jeremy saved my life once. I'm giving you a fighting chance in return."

"You're leaving?"

"Looks like it."

"People will know what you did. There are witnesses who saw us together."

Christian laughs. "They'll never find me. Good luck with your demon. I hope that bitch tears you apart." He clamps down on the gas and speeds away.

How the fuck did he know? What else did he know?

Andy checks her snowmobile. Christian mangled it even before he shot at it. He cut the fucking fuel line.

Andy's stranded. She gathers the weapons she can find—knives and acid, no guns. Then she makes her way to town. She tries to push away the thoughts that she'll die out here. She never should have left. She should have listened when Ava told her not to run. This was a colossally stupid idea. She hasn't been in her right mind since Jeremy died. She wasn't ready for another case.

Ava was right.

Faith was right.

Tristan was right.

Oriana was right.

And Christian knows exactly where to find them. He must have known when he contacted Andy.

Shit.

That must be his plan. He must have needed to lure Andy away. Now all he has to do is wait for Ava to be alone and unguarded.

Then again, Oriana is so strong now. She can defend Ava, if she's still around, if Oriana hasn't left Ava's. But someone as experienced as Christian will know how to overpower Oriana.

She shoves the thought away and tries to conjure the idea of fire and something warm. She doesn't know how long she walks. She only knows she doesn't see the lights of town on the horizon. The wind picks up again, chilling her to the bone. She can't stop. If she stops, she dies.

Over the howl of the wind, she hears a hum behind her. She knows who it is before she turns around.

"Hello, Andy," says a sweet, familiar voice.

Andy grips her knife tighter. She can't afford to fuck up this time.

"I missed you," says the voice.

Andy turns.

Her mother stands not three feet away, barefoot in the snow. After decades she still looks the same. She looks exactly as she did when she tucked Andy into bed the last night before she was possessed.

"I'm very tired of being followed," she says.

Andy's hands shake. Now or never. She has a choice to make and she's running out of time. It's her or the demon.

"If I kill you," she says, "is your little friend going to be my next problem?"

She can't help it. She owes it to Faith to try. "Mom?" whispers Andy.

Her face twists into a grin. "No."

Andy needs to keep her talking if she wants to get to her mother. "Why us? Why did you choose us?"

She moves forward. "I needed a new body. My old body was getting boring. I found your mommy first."

No reason. Just a body. That can't be. Her family wasn't destroyed by *chance*. It wasn't random. It was vengeance, or a plot, or something, anything but chance.

"Did Jeremy tell you?"

Andy's heart sinks into her stomach.

"I bet he didn't tell you. I let him choose which body I took."

"Mom, I know you can hear me."

"Don't do that," says the demon. "That's sad. Ask me what happened."

"Let her go."

"I'll tell you anyway. He begged me to take him. He was ready. So, I picked your mother. He should have seen it coming. I was going to take the opposite of whoever he chose anyway."

"Mom?" says Andy. "It's Andy. I'm your daughter. The demon is going to kill me."

"Stupid girl. I killed her a long time ago."

If she does nothing, the demon is going to kill her. She'll die alone in the dark in the cold. She'll die and it will all be over.

It's her or her mom.

Andy lowers her knife. It slips from her fingers and drops into the snow. What's the point? She's too far away for help to arrive. This is it.

Only one of them gets to walk away from this. Andy's done all she can. She's played her part in the world. No one needs her. If she survives, she'll just go back to trapping, and since meeting Oriana, she knows she doesn't have the stomach for it. Maybe she'll just drink her life away. She's going to die one way or another.

Her or her mom.

She sinks to her knees, takes off her mask and goggles and looks into her mother's eyes one last time.

The demon smiles as she leans over her. She flashes straight, white teeth as she begins to sing. Her eyes are soft at the edges. She holds Andy's head in her hands. Something warm is flowing from her body into the demon's. She can feel it leaving.

The demon burns brighter the longer she stares at Andy.

Andy's never seen a demon drain energy before. She has no idea how long it takes. She's sure her mom will be quick, though. She wouldn't want to hurt Andy. She'll keep her safe.

Andy hears a familiar lullaby and she's not sure if she's humming or singing or if it's some combination of both. She knows she's tired. Her mom's hands are warm. She's not cold anymore. She closes her eyes.

She hears something loud, like an explosion, in the distance. The noise travels over the tundra to where she is enveloped by memories with her mother.

She hears the noise again, closer. Warm hands leave her face. She slumps, boneless, into the snow.

* * *

Andy wakes up in a bed, warm, whole, and dazed. She tests her body by clenching and unclenching her fists. Her joints are stiff, but functional.

"Andy?" Faith rushes to her side. The bed sinks as she sits beside her. She puts a hand on her forehead. "Are you awake?"

She means to say "yes" but just grumbles instead. She slowly opens her eyes. She recognizes her surroundings.

"Easy, you're still weak."

Andy means to say, "no shit."

Faith grins. "How are you feeling?"

Andy frowns. "Shitty." She blinks and pushes herself up.

"Don't overdo it."

Andy ignores her.

Christian's apartment. They're in Christian's apartment. Christian left her. The demon found her. Her mother found her. She snaps her attention to Faith. "Mom? Did you see her?"

Faith bites her lip. "We'll talk about that later. How are you feeling? I've only treated a few energy drains."

"Did you see Mom?"

"Later."

"No, now. Did you see her?"

"Yes."

Andy sits up straighter. "Is she all right? Can you fix her? Is she still in there?"

"Andy, I…she's…" She's broadcasting the truth before she says it. "…I killed her."

Andy leans back down. "She was going to kill you. That wasn't a chance I was willing to take."

Her or Mom. Faith chose her.

Her sister breaks. She's in tears. "I'm sorry. I didn't have a choice."

Andy wraps an arm around her and lets Faith cry into her shoulder.

"What about the body?"

Faith wipes her eyes. "I took care of it."

Something like relief bleeds into her and Andy finally lets herself break too. She cries. Faith apologizes. Andy tries to calm her.

Jeremy would have hated this. He would have wanted to die instead of their mother.

The thought shakes Andy and it takes a minute to settle. Jeremy wanted to die. Jeremy didn't tell Andy that the demon was wearing her mother's body because he wanted Andy to hesitate. He wanted Andy to choose. He wanted Andy to choose her mom.

"I'm sorry," says Faith again.

"It's okay," repeats Andy. For the first time, she thinks she might mean it.

CHAPTER TWENTY

Faith, as it turns out, used the GPS in Jeremy's phone to track her to Alaska. She installed an app on his phone while they were at Ava's. She said she knew Andy would keep the phone nearby.

She'd let Andy get a head start, hoping she'd change her mind and come home. "It was easy to follow you guys," she says. "Once I got here, I followed a trail of unusual activity to Utqiagvik. It helps that Ava still has access to the network."

"How did you find me out there?"

"Your witness. I wish I'd gotten there sooner."

They're seated at the table in the apartment. Christian hasn't returned. Earlier, they called Ava and Tristan to let them know he might come sniffing around. They still haven't heard from Oriana.

Faith insists they stay one more night at the apartment to let Andy rest. Andy uses it as an opportunity to collect information on Christian. He's got pages and pages of notes on angels and demons, but his handwriting is almost impossible to decipher.

"Andy," says Faith, without being prompted, "I want you to know there's nothing wrong with you and Oriana being—you know—together."

Andy looks up from the notes. "What?"

"I think I understand why you freaked out, but you didn't take advantage of Oriana or anything. She likes you."

"She doesn't know any better."

"You've got to stop doing that. You're diminishing her decisions when you act like you know what's best for her. She's damaged, yes, but frankly, so are you. I'm not sure either one of you are in any kind of position to know what's best."

Andy opens her mouth, but Faith gives her a stern look. "Don't. Just shut up and process what I said. You can disagree later, but at least think about it before you throw a fit."

Andy snorts and returns to the notes. "Fine."

"I want to add one more thing."

"No one's stopping you."

"It doesn't matter *why* she was comfortable talking to you. The fact is she *was* comfortable, and she talked, and that helped her heal. I don't know what you did, or why it worked, but the point is, you helped her."

"I guess so."

"And she made you happy."

Andy doesn't reply.

"Ava said she made you happy. You fixed each other and that's—"

"All right, Faith, I get the picture. You can stop bullshitting me."

"If you could just think about it, and maybe consider that it was something she wanted too—"

"I get it. I'll think about it. Please, for Christ's sake, stop talking." She passes a notebook across the table. "Put that giant brain of yours to good use and help me make sense of this nutjob."

They talk almost exclusively about Christian for the rest of the day. Shortly after ten p.m. Faith puts her foot down and demands Andy rests if she wants to head back home in the morning.

Andy falls asleep, imagining the heavy blanket is a large black wing draped over her. She sleeps for fourteen hours. It's a new record for her adult life. Faith stays true to her word, and they set off shortly after Andy wakes up. Her truck is still parked outside of Christian's apartment. Faith actually lets Andy drive alone, and she follows behind her, driving Ava's pickup. Every few hours, Faith honks the horn, signaling time for a break. Andy complies. It makes the trip home twice as long, but it keeps Faith happy, so Andy doesn't complain.

Faith says Andy can keep driving as long as she stops to rest and lets Faith check her vitals. It takes them days to complete the drive. Andy behaves and doesn't pick a fight the entire time. Finally, they get home on a Saturday around one a.m. The lights are on and Ava and Tristan are waiting for them on the porch. Andy's barely out of the car before her family smothers her. Ava scolds her and Tristan says he's glad she and Faith are safe.

Andy watches as he embraces Faith and she feels the tiniest sting of jealousy.

Ava slaps her hard on the back, then drapes an arm over her shoulder. "You could have died!"

"Yeah, I get that a lot," says Andy.

"How do I convince you to stick around?"

"You could try grounding me again."

Ava rolls her eyes. "Don't think I've ruled that out." She tugs Andy's shirt. "C'mon. I've got food and a fire going inside."

They return to the house with Faith and Tristan in tow and gather in the living room, Andy close to the fireplace.

"I'm guessing Christian has all of your stuff," says Tristan.

"Most of it. Anything I didn't leave in the car is with him."

He nods. "Did you have anything about Oriana? Anything that might suggest where she went?"

"I don't think so. He's got both of my phones and my laptop, but I didn't keep anything about Oriana on them." She sinks back into her chair, doing yet another mental inventory of the things she's lost. "He's got my gear. Dad came up with a few gnarly ways to kill mon—angels and demons. I don't know if he shared that info with Christian, but he damn sure knows now."

"Anything we need to be worried about?" asks Faith.

"Holy water's the worst of it," answers Andy. "Dad sold a few batches, but he kept the best for us."

"What else?"

Andy sighs. "Grenades."

"Where the fuck did Dad get grenades?"

"I don't know. Probably the same place he got sodium thiopental and fifty pounds of lye. He knew when to pull rank."

"Did you drag fifty pounds of lye through the Arctic?"

Andy shakes her head. "Nah. We used that up years ago. Still had some sodium thiopental, though. Probably not enough to impact something inhuman. It takes a shit ton to get them to talk. We learned that the hard way. Same goes for lye. Especially with angels. First one we tried to dissolve, we ended up with this fleshy, feathery soup."

Andy still remembers the smell. They ended up sealing the container and locking it in a storage unit. Jeremy said he went back for it, but Andy's not sure if that was true. Someday, someone is going to open that unit and find several gallons of failed holy water along with creature stew. They are in for a nasty surprise, if they haven't uncovered it already. Andy doesn't have her own storage unit, as she always shared Jeremy's. Maybe the creature stew leaked and ate everything else.

"We went back to slicing them up after that," says Andy. Her chest is tight. She doesn't know why she's still talking. "Ava, your chop shop had nothing on us. We got it down to an art."

The others are watching her in silence.

"We'd lay out a monster"—Andy spreads her arms wide to demonstrate—"and go to town. We'd build the pyre in the same spot, then bury the evidence once it was over."

Andy rests her head against her fist and stares into the fireplace. "Granted, we had to kill the thing first. God, that took forever. Faith, I'm sure you remember. We got better after you quit, but our last kill took thirty minutes. That's not including Mom, of course. We didn't kill her, so it doesn't count. It took her a few seconds to kill Dad."

No one stops her from talking, so she keeps going.

"I didn't tell you guys that, but the demon that possessed Mom is the thing that killed Dad. I hesitated and bam!" She snaps her fingers. "Dead." It's not so bad now that she says it out loud. Or maybe she's zoned out. Either way it doesn't hurt.

Faith glances to Tristan.

"There was this big angel. She had these huge wings, and they were so white. She was gorgeous. We found her living in fucking Boston of all places. Just hanging out, pretending to be human. She gave herself away, though. She couldn't resist the urge to fly. I guess it's in their DNA or something. Oriana is like that too—she has to fly."

Faith says something quietly. Ava stands and steps out of Andy's line of sight.

"Anyway," says Andy, "we see her land in this nice quiet park. It's a new moon. There's one working streetlight. We can't see for shit. She was in an area with other humans so Dad and I blended right in...she couldn't sense us. We fired off a couple shots...I aimed for the torso and Dad got her wings. That was standard procedure. We had to inflict a massive amount of damage so the monsters wouldn't be able to heal as fast. If you could get the clearance for a headshot, that was the best. God there was a lot of blood. There was always so much blood."

Something warm and wet trickles down the side of her cheek. She wipes it away. "We dumped gallons of water in the grass to get rid of the blood. Found out later I hit an artery in her leg—I was a crap shot—we had to wrap her up in a tarp and some of those clear plastic paint mats to keep her from bleeding all over the car." She runs a hand over her face and takes a shaky breath. "I was so fucking glad that job was over. I took a feather. Gave it to Oriana, though. We burned a whole bunch of stuff—mine and Christian's."

Ava moves to stand beside her.

"Trophies," says Andy, almost choking. "It wasn't really our stuff. It was just a bunch of trophies. Christian and I both had trophies. Did you guys see Oriana's dad's wings? I don't know who mounted them, but damn, they did a great job. I've never seen wings stuffed like that before. When I first saw Oriana lying outside that cabin, I was going to hack off her wings and hang them up somewhere." She takes another breath. "I think Christian did the same with Oriana's dad's wings."

She can't shut herself up. She's tired. Maybe that's the problem. Faith was right. She should have rested more.

"You know how much that would have fucked Oriana up? The only thing keeping her going was the idea she might be able to fly again. Then when she did, shit, she was a new woman. She's *got* to have her wings. You can't take wings from an angel."

Ava's kneeling by her chair, her hand is heavy on Andy's shoulder.

"We always did. Standard procedure. If you see wings, cut them down. We fucked them up."

Faith is watching her. "Andy?"

Tristan is quietly observing.

"Fucked up," mutters Andy. She's said too much. She can tell by the look on Faith's face. She shouldn't have started talking. "I guess you all know Christian was the one who had Oriana imprisoned. I didn't know he knew Dad, but I guess you knew that. I guess that's why you didn't tell me." She huffs. "I don't blame you."

"You're not like him," says Ava. She squeezes her shoulder.

Andy tries to laugh it off, but it comes out as a strangled sob. "Sorry, I've been breaking down a lot these days."

"Don't be sorry," says Ava. "That's good. You need to talk about this shit. We've all done bad. I was in your shoes when Faith came to me and said she wanted to stop killing and start saving. I'm not saying forgive yourself. I haven't even figured out how to do that yet, but you've got to stop reliving it."

Andy looks up at Faith, who says, "I killed Mom."

"You had to."

Tristan doesn't contribute. Violence never touched his life. He stayed above the waves in a sea of horrors and was able to pull Faith up when she drifted across his path. Andy pulled her back down. That can't happen again. She's got a family now. If she sinks, they'll all go down with her.

CHAPTER TWENTY-ONE

Oriana's nightmare woke the entire house. Josiah joins them in the living room once Dina is asleep again and takes a seat beside Oriana. Tabbris and Lailah are sitting side by side, bleary-eyed and impatient. Oriana doesn't know when they arrived.

"We can begin," says Ariel. She's standing in the center of the room, eyes locked on Oriana. "We need to be on the lookout for another human—a trapper."

"Let me guess," says Josiah, he shoots Oriana a look. "Andy."

She sinks lower into her chair. The room is watching her. No secrets, not when she could be putting Dina at risk. She recites her history again, beginning with her first escape attempt from Ava's, and this time she includes Andy.

Midway through explaining her night in the cabin, Josiah interrupts, "Ariel, I don't think we need to make her tell us all this stuff."

"I want to hear more," says Lailah.

"Me too," says Tabbris.

"Majority rules," says Ariel.

"But look at her. She's all fidgety and pale."

"It's all right," says Oriana.

Josiah glares at the others. "Who's using auras?"

"No one," answers Oriana. "I am speaking on my own free will."

She does her best to accurately explain the relationship. Ariel demands a meticulous analysis of Andy's emotional state. Oriana finally reaches the end and finishes with the fight. The angels stay silent when she finishes the story.

Ariel is scowling but seems lost in thought as she stares her down. Josiah has his head bowed and his arms crossed. Lailah and Tabbris exchange a look that could only be described as guilty.

Oriana catches Tabbris's eye. He sighs. "What's Andy look like?"

Ariel and Josiah snap out of their trances at the same time.

"Why?" asks Oriana.

"It might be relevant."

It's quick, but Oriana sees the look Ariel and Josiah exchange.

"You know her," says Oriana.

"It depends on what she looks like," says Tabbris.

"That's enough," snaps Ariel.

Oriana stands. "How do you know her?"

"Just tell her," says Lailah.

"No," snaps Ariel.

"Pretty sure it's too late," says Josiah.

"Ariel sent us to find your trapper," says Lailah, "the bad one."

Ariel doesn't object this time. She watches Oriana for a reaction.

"We think we found him," says Lailah. "He's still active so we were able to find him by finding other enochs. We found this guy up in Alaska. We think it might be your kidnapper."

"And?" asks Oriana.

Ariel glares at the two angels. "That was supposed to be a secret."

"Why?" asks Oriana. "And what does that have to do with Andy?"

Ariel rubs her temples. "It was...sometimes it is necessary to...Some people are better off dead."

"Damn, Ariel," says Josiah. "Way to ease her into it."

"A person like that is not doing the world any good," says Ariel.

"Nobody's arguing with you," says Josiah.

"He's mine to kill," says Oriana.

"We didn't want you to have to make that decision," says Ariel. "We know you are struggling to find the goodness in yourself. It is easier, and potentially healthier for you, if we take care of it."

"No," says Oriana. "I want to do it."

"She's got a blood grudge," says Tabbris. "I think we should let her do it."

"I second that," says Josiah.

"Third," says Lailah.

"Fine," mutters Ariel.

"How did you find him?" asks Oriana.

"We've got connections," says Lailah. "And auras help, too." Before Ariel can protest, Lailah adds, "We were gentle. Just like you asked."

Oriana rubs her forehead. It is just her luck that someone else would find her captor before her.

"As for Andy," says Tabbris, "the trapper we found has a little friend with him."

Oriana's heart skips a beat. "Andy?"

"I don't know," says Tabbris. "Again, that depends on what she looks like."

"She's a few inches taller than I am," says Oriana. "I know her age is thirty-something, but I cannot remember exactly. She always has this grumpy look on her face but I don't think she's actually always grumpy."

Tabbris and Lailah exchange another glance.

"What?" asks Oriana.

Lailah wrinkles her nose. "Well," she begins. "Someone we identified as Andrea Black is with him. I think they're working together."

"Take me to them."

"You're not ready," says Ariel.

Oriana is already on her feet. She can feel her aura burning within her. She reaches out to Tabbris with it. "Take me to them," she commands.

Tabbris's face goes slack for just a second.

Oriana feels her power tug, then snap. She staggers back.

"Ariel's right," he says, coming back around. "You're not ready."

"More importantly," says Lailah, "we don't know why Andy and Christian are together."

Christian.

Oriana mouths the name but doesn't say it out loud. She straightens up to her full height and faces Ariel. "If you will not take me to them, I will find them on my own."

"Just because your human is with him?" asks Ariel.

"He is a cruel man. You don't know what he is capable of."

"And you don't know why Andy is with him," says Josiah. He stands and crosses the room, positioning himself beside Ariel.

"Andy most likely intends to kill him," says Oriana.

"They looked pretty chummy together," says Tabbris.

"Yeah," agrees Lailah. "We watched them for a while. It's just the two of them. Andy's had plenty of opportunity to kill the bastard, if that's what she was planning."

Oriana clenches her jaw. The room blurs in and out of focus as she replays her last conversation with Andy. She's still a trapper. That's what Andy was trying to say. She was confessing. Andy's loyalty to her sister was the only thing that kept her from killing Oriana, and Andy knew she wouldn't be able to maintain the illusion much longer. She didn't feel anything. Andy was right. Oriana was delusional.

Stupid monster.

But it all felt real.

"You know what," says Josiah, disturbing the silence, "fuck it. We'll all go."

"Absolutely not," says Ariel.

"All in favor, raise your hand," says Josiah.

Ariel folds her arms as hands shoot up around her.

"Majority rules," says Josiah.

"I'm pulling rank," says Ariel.

Josiah groans. "Don't do that."

"We can't leave Dina," says Ariel.

"You can stay with her," says Josiah. He kneels. "Please? I'm literally begging on my knees. It's been years since I've been this curious about something."

Ariel glares down, unmoved.

Tabbris and Lailah are quick to join Josiah's pleading.

"Please?" asks Lailah. "In the name of vengeance. I want to smite something."

"Or justice," says Tabbris, "whichever you prefer."

"They can't take down three angels and a hybrid," says Josiah. "We're strong. Overpowered even."

"That's what bothers me," mutters Ariel. She pinches the bridge of her nose. "Get up, you look ridiculous."

"Does that mean we can go? Did we wear you down?"

"You have hours, not days. You go, do whatever you need to do, make sure you don't get caught, then come right back."

"Permission to let Oriana kill Christian?" asks Tabbris.

"And Andy, if she deserves it?" asks Lailah.

"Recon only," says Ariel, "and if you're not back soon, I'm calling in every favor I have with every angel I know to haul your asses back here."

"I call dibs on patrol leader," says Tabbris.

"Josiah is in charge," says Ariel. "He's most familiar with the area."

"He doesn't know Alaska," says Tabbris.

"Neither do you," says Ariel. "Ground rules, since this involves emotional bonds and another human, no killing or fighting. Defend and retreat should conflict arise. Do not leave Oriana alone. Actually, no one gets left alone. You stay together."

"Can we reveal ourselves?" asks Josiah.

"No. Do you understand the terms?"

"Yes," answers Josiah. "And we accept. We'll leave now, if it's all the same to you."

"I'm ready," says Oriana.

"Good," says Ariel. "Josiah's in charge. Lailah is his second. Tabbris will guard Oriana. Your clock begins counting down as soon as you leave."

They take off just before sunrise. The angels help Oriana fly faster toward somewhere cold and very dark.

"Welcome to Alaska," says Josiah.

Oriana makes a mental note to investigate a world map when she returns. "Where is Christian?"

"Heading north, last time we checked," answers Tabbris. "We might have to fly around a bit before we find him again."

"Lead the way," says Oriana.

As it turns out, flying around a bit is easier said than done. It's several hours before they pick up Christian's trail again. Tabbris says it was easier when he and Lailah were searching because they split up to cover more ground. Josiah makes them stay together, threatening to tell Ariel if they don't.

They stop by every hotel and gas station along the way, usually sending in Lailah with her wings cloaked, to show Christian's picture to the person inside. They follow several thin leads to a cold town where the highway ends.

The others cloak their wings but are careful to stay masked in the darkness with Oriana. Josiah says it stays dark for a while in this part of the world. It's a small blessing since it's easier for them to stay hidden.

"They've got to be here somewhere," says Lailah. "This is literally the end of the road."

"Unless they went back," says Tabbris. "Or took a plane. We should check for their car. If they're still in town, we don't want to tip them off that we're asking around about them."

It doesn't take long to find the car. It's parked in a lot in front of a hotel. They peek inside. Oriana spots a small black feather hanging from a mirror attached to the windshield. Josiah has to pull her away.

"They're still here," breathes Oriana. She can feel Andy. She doesn't understand how, but she can feel her. She can feel her kidnapper too. A familiar dread snakes through her.

Josiah nods to Lailah. "See if you can figure out which room they're in."

Oriana stares up at the hotel. Andy is inside. Andy is with Christian. They're on an expedition together.

Andy's mother. They must be looking for her mother. But Andy said that was personal. It was something she wanted to do alone. Why would she involve Christian? Maybe they are not tracking Andy's mother. Maybe they are tracking something else. Her mind is racing, struggling to create a story.

Lailah returns and startles Oriana.

"Found them," she says. "It's pretty quiet inside, we should be able to sneak to their room."

"Which window is theirs?" asks Oriana.

"It's around the other side."

"Show me."

Lailah leads them to the back of the hotel. They're careful to avoid the lights. The wind picks up and the howl covers any sounds they make. Oriana's skin prickles, but she realizes she's not cold. Her aura kicked in at some point, instinctively keeping her warm. It's never done that before.

They locate the trappers' window. It's near the ground and they don't need to fly to peer inside. Oriana steps up first. She's breathing so hard she's dizzy. She presses her face to the window. She can see inside through a gap in the curtain.

Andy is curled up on her side facing the window, asleep. Christian is sleeping in the bed just a few feet away. Andy isn't being restrained. She's frowning slightly and Oriana recognizes her unrest as a nightmare.

Each of them has a bag. Andy's laptop is on the floor by her bed. She's not a hostage. She's here willingly. Lailah and Tabbris said they were traveling in the same vehicle. Andy must have seen the feather in the car. She must at least be suspicious of Christian.

Oriana doesn't realize her hands are sparking with aura until Josiah pulls her away from the window.

"You all right?"

Oriana nods. She tries to think of something other than shattering the glass and bursting into the room. Her fingertips are burning. "I need to go home," she says.

She wants to show herself. She wants to wake Andy and ask her what she's doing. *Why* she's doing it. She needs answers, but she's so afraid of hearing her fears confirmed she's reluctant to move. No one questions her. Each angel places a hand on her and the cold, dark landscape disappears.

CHAPTER TWENTY-TWO

Andy is on a steady dose of medication with a name she can't pronounce. Faith insists she take it and has zero sympathy when Andy whines about it tasting like chalk. At least she's not stuck inside anymore. The four of them are on a mission. It feels good to have Faith riding shotgun in her car again. Ava and Tristan are following behind them in the truck.

Ava got a call yesterday. A trapper near Seattle wanted to know if he had any information on an angel in a female body with large black wings. The trapper said he and several others encountered the angel a few weeks ago. He said the angel was manic and searching for information on another trapper. Ava sent the guy toward Colorado on a false lead.

That was all the information they had in terms of locating Oriana, but it had at least confirmed their suspicions that she was in Washington looking for Christian. They'd left the next morning, encouraged by the report.

Faith keeps trying to convince Andy that it's not her fault Oriana ran away, but that's a load of crap. It's absolutely Andy's fault. If she'd kept her stupid mouth shut, none of this would have happened.

Andy doesn't care who they find first. If it's Oriana, she'll apologize—beg, plead, bribe—whatever it takes to get her to come back so they can keep her safe. If they find Christian first, Andy's not going to hesitate this time. She's going to shoot the son of a bitch in the head and call it a goddamn day.

Faith's phone rings and she answers it. "Hey, Tristan, need us to pull over?"

Andy can hear his muffled voice on the other end of the call but can't make out what he's saying.

"Condolences for what?" asks Faith. "Are you fucking kidding me?" She glances at Andy, mouth parted as if she's about to start shouting. "What did Ava say?"

"What's going on?" asks Andy.

Faith holds up a hand. "That's probably the best way to play it—yeah—yeah I'll tell her." She hangs up the phone. "Ava just got a call from a friend of yours. He called to offer his condolences because he heard you were dead."

"Motherfucker."

"Christian must be talking. I guess he thinks you're dead."

"Or he's making sure I'm dead. If he spreads the word and someone's seen me alive, he's assuming they'll correct him." Andy grips the steering wheel a little harder than necessary.

"Tristan said Ava played along, so we're covered there."

"Or he's just trying to fuck with us. I don't like that they called Ava."

"Maybe he's plotting."

"I don't know, but he was a friend of Dad's. That should tell you all you need to know about him. He's nuts, and he knows what you do and didn't hesitate to threaten me."

"You're spiraling."

"He's got to die." Andy glares at the road.

"One thing at a time. There's no point worrying about it now. Let's just focus on finding Oriana."

"Oriana is probably already dead. If she was running around flashing her wings all over Seattle—of all fucking places—

somebody probably already took her out. Maybe Christian already found her We're probably too late."

"Andy, we talked about this."

"I should have minded my own fucking business."

"If you don't calm down, I'm going to make you ride with Tristan."

Andy continues to glare at the road. The car is too damn slow and there's too much traffic. It's too hot and her chest is too tight.

Start with what you know.

Christian must have been a close friend of Jeremy's, otherwise he wouldn't know about her mom. He made it back alive from the Arctic because how else would the rumor spread about Andy's death? The fact that he didn't return to Fairbanks isn't a good sign. It means he's suspicious, paranoid, or he knew Faith and Andy were staying there.

"Slow down," says Faith.

"What?"

"You're pushing one hundred. Slow down. Ava can't keep up."

Andy eases off the gas and checks behind her. Ava and Tristan are trying to catch up.

The sighting could be bait. This whole thing could be a trap. They'll reach Seattle tomorrow. That gives Christian plenty of time to prepare.

Andy tries to convince them to drive through the night and arrive early. Ava puts her foot down outside of Missoula and makes them stop for the night. Andy and Ava share a room and Faith and Tristan share a room.

Ava hits the bed as soon as they bring their bags in, but Andy sets up Ava's computer at the table and starts looking for anything that might point to Oriana. She's got about fifteen tabs open and not a single lead. She's not even sure what she's looking for. She uses Ava's ID number to access the tracking site.

Ava grumbles something from the bed. A few moments later, without warning, she sits down beside Andy and puts a bottle on the table between them. She pours Andy a glass and sets it loudly in the space between her and the laptop.

"Drink that. Calm the hell down, give your brain a rest and go to sleep."

"Thought I had to detox," says Andy, pushing the glass away.

"I thought so too, but I didn't know this was the alternative."

Andy grunts and opens a new tab. Someone spotted a "large birdlike creature" flying over Olympia weeks ago. It made the news.

Christian couldn't fake that. Not unless he's got connections. That's possible. Jeremy made connections everywhere he went, but then again Jeremy wasn't an abrasive psychopath.

Ava trades the glass for two pills and a bottle of water. "Faith said I'm in charge of making you take your meds."

Andy pops the pills in her mouth, but immediately spits them out. "What's this?" She holds up the second pill.

"Half an Ambien."

Andy pops her usual chalk-tasting pill and swallows it. She pushes the Ambien off to the side.

"If you don't sleep, you can't drive tomorrow."

"One more hour."

"You can go to bed now or I can call in your sister and we'll hold you down and inject you with horse tranquilizer and make you go to bed."

She says something else, but Andy ignores her. Ava threatens her again over the next few minutes but doesn't follow through.

Andy knew she wouldn't. At some point, Ava gives up and goes to sleep. Andy keeps searching until the sun peeks through the curtains. She hasn't made any progress. There are no recent sightings.

Everything even remotely related to angel activity is old news. They're just going to drive around the Pacific Northwest following a trail of vague sightings until they give up or walk into Christian's trap. Either way, they don't stand a chance of finding Oriana.

It's morning. Ava is milling around the room. She finishes her coffee then takes her bag to the car. Andy didn't even bother bringing in anything. She stares at the screen until Ava shouts that they're ready to get back on the road. Andy shuts the laptop, tucks it under her arm and goes outside. She stops in front of her car. Faith is behind the wheel and Ava is in the truck with her.

Faith pulls out of the parking space while Andy is still banging on the window. She almost throws the laptop on the ground in her frustration. Instead, she gets into the truck with Tristan.

"One hour," she says, "then I drive."

"Whatever you need to tell yourself," says Tristan.

Andy tucks the laptop behind her seat and sits with her arms firmly crossed.

"Ava said you didn't sleep last night."

"I went to sleep after she did and woke up before she did."

"Yeah, right."

"Are you going to drive this slow the whole way?"

"I'm not going to go faster than Faith, if that's what you're asking."

"Just saying, we could shave an hour off the drive time if you'd speed up."

"We have plenty of time."

Andy leans back and presses against the headrest.

"Faith says you're worried Christian might be planning something."

"Did you guys have a meeting or something this morning?"

"You get angrier the closer we get to finding Oriana. Why is that?"

"Not going to turn this into a session, Tristan."

"Is it because you're worried she's dead and it's your fault?"

Andy doesn't answer.

"Why did you tell her she had Stockholm syndrome?"

"Tristan," warns Andy.

"Were you trying to push her away?"

"If I go to sleep, will you leave me alone?"

Tristan has the nerve to laugh at her. "The last patient I had to negotiate like this with was Oriana."

"Lot of good that did."

"You're right. She was only willing to talk to you."

Andy bites her lip. Oriana trusted her more than she ever deserved to be trusted.

"Do you think she felt like she could relate to you?"

"I was just familiar."

"Because you were a trapper?"

"*Am* a trapper, and yes."

"You don't think it was just because you, as a person, make her feel safe?"

"I promised to kill her if she hadn't healed in two weeks."

"Tell me about that."

Andy glances at him. He's trying to hide it, but she can tell he's surprised. She smirks, feeling a weird sense of victory at having shaken him. "She asked me to kill her. I knew that would piss Faith off, so I told her to think about it for two weeks. If she still wanted to die, I'd pull the trigger."

"What did you think might change in two weeks?"

"It gave her time to heal and gave me time to come up with a plan."

"Obviously you didn't kill her. Did she want to die?"

"No. Once her wings healed, she changed her mind."

"Ava said you let her ride in the truck to practice flying."

"Yeah," mutters Andy. She resumes scowling at the road.

"Why would you do that?"

"I don't know."

"Did it make her happy?"

"Seemed to."

"Did you know it would make her happy?"

"She's half-angel. Angels like flying. It's not rocket science."

"Did you think making her happy would make her want to live?"

"Happy people typically don't have a death wish. Then again, I'm no expert."

"Why did you care if she wanted to live?"

Andy rubs a hand over her face. "I didn't want to kill her. Meant a lot to Faith to keep her alive and Faith means a lot to me."

"You could have just refused to kill her. You didn't have to try to change her mind."

"She would've just tried to hurt herself."

"You could have told Ava. You two could have made sure she couldn't kill herself. You didn't have to keep her secret."

"Yeah," mutters Andy.

"But you did."

"So?"

"Why?"

"I don't know." She focuses on the bumper of her truck cruising along ahead of them. "It wasn't my secret to tell."

"So, you respect her."

"I guess."

"Have you considered that she likes you because you are kind and because you understand her?"

"Oriana grew up in a goddamn grain silo with a lunatic who was keeping her like an animal. She's not a great judge of character."

"You're projecting your own self-hatred. That's not fair to her. When we find her, let her like you."

"*If* we find her."

"*When* we find her."

Andy hesitates. "You'll make sure she's okay—that I don't hurt her?"

"Yes."

Andy sighs. "All right."

Out of the corner of her eye she can see Tristan smiling to himself. She's not sure what she just agreed to, but at least she can count on him for backup. She probably should have talked to him a long time ago. Faith's going to be so smug when she finds out.

CHAPTER TWENTY-THREE

Every day Ariel asks about Andy and every day Oriana says it doesn't bother her. Andy's human and Oriana's not surprised. Every day Oriana spars with the other angels and every day she improves. Every day she becomes faster, stronger, more like the others, and every night she sees Andy sleeping in that room with Christian.

Oriana steps outside, wings flexed and ready, aura sparking at her fingertips. Ariel stands across from her. Her eyes are closed. She's listening, waiting for her to move first.

She'd outmatched Tabbris quickly. It was easy. Tabbris never paid enough attention to the fight. Lailah took longer, but eventually Oriana realized she couldn't match her stamina. Oriana was able to consistently tire her out and win the match.

Josiah was much harder. He'd taken it easy against Oriana before. When he unleashed his full power, Oriana was certain she'd never be able to defeat him. They could spar for hours without Josiah breaking a sweat. Ariel had said confidence was his weakness, but as far as Oriana could tell, Josiah had every right to be confident. He seemed unstoppable.

The day she progressed she went in expecting to lose again. She flew high in retreat. Josiah surged forward and grabbed one of Oriana's wings, rerouting them both to the ground. Oriana snapped. She lunged and was met with a barrage of attacks, but her power and her mind were on autopilot. She didn't think to fall back. Instead, she fought.

Ariel had to intervene.

Josiah and Oriana had landed, soaked in sweat and blood with auras struggling to mend their injuries.

Ariel had healed them both and Josiah had shaken her hand. That night, Josiah had told her to pay attention to her triggers and what made her disassociate and to use that in their next fight. She did and she won. The angels agreed it was time for her to face Ariel.

"Your strength is her weakness," shouts Josiah as he and the others gather to watch. Dina is peeking through her fingers.

"That doesn't make any sense," says Tabbris.

"This feels kind of unfair," says Lailah.

"She can handle herself," says Josiah.

"I take it back," says Lailah. "She's not ready."

Oriana tries to ignore them. She needs Ariel to move. As soon as she feels that first swell of pain, she can tune the world out and let her body go.

When Josiah grabbed her wing, her mind went back to the silo. Pain didn't register. Thanks to her training, her power took over. She's been able to use that to her advantage in every match since. She hopes it will have the same effect against Ariel.

Across from her, Ariel launches into the air. Oriana can hear her wings as she circles above her, but she can't see her.

Josiah is shouting from the sidelines, "Boo, Ariel! Knock her out, Oriana!"

She dives from the sky and Oriana is too stunned to remember she's supposed to strike. Ariel touches two fingers to her forehead and that's the last thing she sees. When she comes around again, Josiah is the one with a hand over his face.

"You can't get distracted," says Ariel.

"I wasn't," mutters Oriana. She sits up, expecting to be lightheaded, but she's surprisingly fine.

"You have an advantage fighting the others. You see the same strategy every day. You know what to expect the next day. You have a chance to prepare. In a real battle, you will not have that advantage. Consider yourself lucky."

"If it's any consolation," says Josiah, "Ariel used the same tender, gentle method when she trained me."

Ariel helps Oriana stand. "Another round?"

"Yes," she answers.

Ariel speeds around again, disorienting her. For her last trick, she dives quickly and appears behind her and wraps her arms around Oriana's torso, pinning her arms to her sides. Oriana blacks out again.

It takes several days before she even manages to land a punch.

* * *

Oriana is demoted to fighting Josiah again until she wins more reliably against him. Unfortunately, as she grows stronger, so does her opponent. Josiah wins the matches when they don't tie.

Instead of hand-to-hand combat, Ariel teaches her to use aura. She trains her and Dina together. Before their morning lesson, Ariel asks again about Andy.

"It doesn't bother me," says Oriana.

After their lesson and before her sparring match, Josiah also asks about Andy.

Oriana gives the same answer.

"I need you to be honest," he says.

"I assure you, it doesn't bother me."

"You're not mad?"

"I'm surprised, but I'm also not going to dwell on it."

"What's going to happen when we go looking for Christian—"

"When *I* go looking for Christian."

"What are you going to do if Andy's with him?"

"Kill Christian. Andy's presence makes no difference."

"Are you willing to kill Andy too?"

She avoids Josiah's inquisitive stare. "Have you found them? Is that why you're asking?"

"Tabbris tracked Christian down again."

Oriana perks up. "He found him?"

"Yeah, well. It's—fuck—okay, Ariel said not to tell you yet, but I think you need to know." Josiah rubs the back of his neck. "Tabbris played human and questioned a few trappers in order to find Christian."

"And?"

"And he asked about Andy." Josiah winces and bites his lip.

"Get to the point."

"He got mixed answers, so maybe it's not true, but a couple of them said Andy died back in Alaska."

Oriana's heart skips a beat. She's aware of Josiah, but only in the sense that she's aware the sky is blue.

"I'm sorry. I should have told you sooner. We wanted to confirm it first—well, everyone else did. I thought you should be in the loop. Maybe that was the wrong call."

Oriana might be staring at him. She's not sure.

"Say something."

"How long?"

"How long what?"

"How long have you known. Did you search for a body? Do you have any idea when she died?"

"We're not sure. Tabbris said the people he talked to heard it secondhand. He and I went to Alaska to see if we could find, um, evidence, but we didn't have much luck."

"So, her body is still out there?"

"She might not even be dead. We're not sure."

"Christian killed her," she says. She needs to talk to Ava. She needs to know more.

"Or whatever they were tracking killed her, or maybe she's still alive. The point is we don't have proof one way or another. I just really thought you should—what are you doing?"

Oriana spreads her wings and launches into the sky.

Josiah is close behind her. "Wait," he calls.

Oriana hears a muffled curse.

Josiah tries to grab her, but Oriana kicks him away. She pushes herself to fly faster and taps into her aura. Suddenly, the wind gushes forward and the breath is knocked out of her. She realizes she's much farther than she was a moment ago. She's beyond the island and the sea and is already flying over the mainland. Emboldened, she pushes herself again and this time she is aware of her power responding. She covers another large amount of distance.

Josiah isn't behind her anymore.

* * *

It takes her a while to find Seattle so she can orient herself, but once she does, she knows where she's going. She retraces her flight path back to Ava's home. It's a much faster trip this time. She spots the property as she flies lower. She braces for a hasty landing, but something grabs her ankle and immobilizes her. She dangles above the trees, supported by a firm grip.

"Idiot," says Ariel.

Oriana cranes her neck to see her and Josiah hovering above her. To her surprise, they do not force her back to the island. The three land among the trees and Ariel releases Oriana.

"What the hell was your plan?" asks Josiah.

"That was reckless," says Ariel. "Do you know how worried we were?"

"How did you—"

"You are predictable," says Ariel.

Oriana begins to defend herself, but something familiar catches her attention. She feels drawn to the house. "Human," she breathes.

"Oh shit," mutters Josiah. "Here we go."

"I warned you," hisses Ariel. "You shouldn't have told her anything."

Oriana hushes them. She creeps from the tree line to get a better view of the house. All the lights are on, but there is an unfamiliar car in the driveway. The trapper is alone inside.

"Wait here," whispers Oriana.

"No," begins Ariel.

"I promise I will call for you if I need help," says Oriana. "I need to try to do this alone. Please."

Josiah nods and holds Ariel's arm. Both seem reluctant to let her go, but they don't follow her. Oriana stalks forward, up the driveway and to the front porch. She can hear movement inside. Glass smashes against the floor and something heavy falls. There is a recognizable scent in the air.

Gasoline.

That's all the motivation she needs. Her hands are burning with aura, and the heat quickly spreads through her body. She holds up one hand and the door splinters into hundreds of tiny pieces.

Christian is standing in the middle of the room, a gas container in his hands. He drops it and reaches behind him for a weapon. Oriana lunges as Christian retrieves his gun. He manages to shoot off one bullet. It lodges in Oriana's shoulder. It doesn't even hurt. Oriana has him by the wrist. She snaps the bones, and the gun falls to the floor. She grabs Christian's other hand and crushes it within her own.

He screams.

Oriana grabs him by the throat and lifts him off the ground. "This is easier than I'd anticipated."

All those wasted years. She believed she was powerless for so long. She imagined this fight over and over and each time, Christian beat her to within inches of her life. She imagined it would take every bit of her strength to defeat him.

But she's become so much more than a creature in a cage. She lowers him to the ground, hand still firmly gripping his neck. "Did you kill anyone in this house?" He smirks and Oriana tightens her grip, allowing her power to flow into the human. "Answer me!"

He shakes his head.

"Did you kill Andy Black?"

"The demon killed her."

"What demon?"

"Her mother."

"Do you know who I am?"

He nods.

"Say my name."

"Oriana," he chokes.

"Good." Oriana positions both of her hands on either side of Christian's face. "This is finished," she says. With that, she twists hard. She hears the harsh crack of bone on bone, and she releases him, letting him fall to the floor. She grabs one of his ankles and drags the body back through the house and outside, where Josiah and Ariel wait.

CHAPTER TWENTY-FOUR

Andy is hunched over Ava's laptop. There are no sightings and none of the trappers in the area have seen Oriana again.

She scrolls through Ava's email. They aren't letting her drive anymore because Ava says she goes too fast.

That's fine with Andy. She's been collecting newspapers from every town they visit. She combs through them when they're in the car.

Ava has several new messages. Most of them are from trappers asking for help on a case or replying and saying they haven't seen a dark-haired woman with black wings. Another email comes through. It's from Ava, to Ava. Andy opens it.

Hello Ava,

I am writing to you from your account, as I do not have an email address of my own. I am currently in your home. I am using one of your computers. I hope you do not mind. We were not able to find your phone number.

I have some unpleasant news. The trapper who held me captive, Christian, broke into your home. He destroyed some of your belongings.

I am here with some new friends, and we have cleaned up most of the mess. I need to speak with you. It is a matter of some urgency.
  Your friend,
  Oriana
"Ava!" shouts Andy.

Ava jerks awake and struggles with her blanket. "What?"

"Oriana." Andy points at the screen.

Ava hurries over and leans in to read the email. "Well I'll be damned," she mutters. "Write her back and tell her to answer the house phone when it rings."

Andy shoots off a reply. *Calling you now. Answer the house phone.*

Ava puts the phone on speaker and sets it on the table. It's ringing. There's a sound as someone answers it.

"Ava Black's house, Josiah speaking."

There's a muffled thump, then another voice speaks.

"Ava? This is Oriana. Where are you? Are you well?"

"Yeah," answers Ava. "God, it's good to hear from you. We're out in Washington trying to track you down."

Andy grabs Ava's arm and whispers, "Don't mention me." Oriana left because of Andy. She might leave again.

Ava gives her a look but nods anyway. "Are you safe?"

"Yes. Christian is dead, and your home is mostly restored. I am here with two angels." A pause. "We are still not sure how to remove the gasoline from the carpet."

"Christian is dead?"

"Yes, I killed him. It was over quickly. Are the others safe?"

"Yeah, we're all fine. We're just worried about you."

"When will you return?"

Andy hits Ava in the arm. "Now," she whispers. "Right now." She notices that Oriana hasn't mentioned her yet.

Ava rolls her eyes. "We'll head back as soon as I wake up the others."

"Good. Would you like us to stay here and guard your home?"

"Don't let her leave," breathes Andy.

"Yeah, that would be great. Thanks."

"It is a two-day journey, correct?"

"Yeah."

"All right. I will look for you in a few days."

Andy has an idea at the last minute. "Ask her what I wrote to her in Enochian that first day," she whispers. "Make sure it's really her."

Ava nods. "Hey, Oriana, what did Andy write in Enochian after we brought you back to the house?"

"'What's your name?'"

"That's right," whispers Andy.

"Okay," says Ava. "Thanks. Just needed to make sure you're really you."

"I am me."

Andy can almost see her frowning in confusion.

"See you soon," says Ava.

"Goodbye."

"Bye." Ava hangs up the phone.

Andy double-checks to make sure the call is over before she speaks. "She's okay."

"And my house is full of angels."

Andy relaxes back into a chair. She's grinning ear to ear. She's back. Oriana met other angels. Oriana will be waiting when they get home. Oriana is safe.

They leave as soon as everyone is awake and packed, but they don't make the trip in one shot. Andy agrees not to whine about stopping if Ava will let her drive the rest of the way home. Ava agrees and adds that Andy has to sleep.

They're on day two of their journey home.

Andy rallies the troops and gets them back to the road. She and Faith take her truck again. Andy drives and speeds the whole way home. They reach the house just before lunchtime. She sees three angels standing in the front lawn. One has massive black wings. She parks the car in front of them and makes eye contact with Oriana through the windshield.

Oriana doesn't look happy, but she doesn't take off, so Andy considers it a small victory. She's practiced her apology the whole way here. She knows how to make this right. She scrambles out of the car and approaches Oriana.

The male angel standing at Oriana's side steps forward, and without warning, socks Andy hard in the jaw.

"Goddamn it!"

"Josiah," shouts the female angel.

Oriana touches her fingers to Andy's jaw. It burns for just a second, then the pain is gone.

"I thought you were dead," says Oriana.

"I'm alive."

A car door slams behind her then her family is at her side.

"What the hell was that for?" demands Faith. She's glaring at Josiah.

"Nice to meet you, too."

"Why did you hit her?"

"Because she deserved it. Ask her why she was with Christian."

Andy's still staring at Oriana. "How did you know about that?"

"We—they—were tracking him. We saw you together in Alaska."

"He threatened me," says Andy quickly. "He said he'd tell people about Ava and Faith and their rehab business. I didn't want a mob of angry trappers coming after them. I was going to let him lead me to the demon and then let it kill him." Oriana seems to be listening, but Andy has no idea if she believes her. "I'm sorry. I should've shot him on sight. I was being stupid."

"You said you wanted to face the demon alone," says Oriana.

"I—shit—yeah I did say that. I'm sorry. I knew better. I wasn't thinking straight. I—I was…I don't know. I was fucked-up. I'm always fucked-up. I'm sorry." Without fail, her practiced apology falls to pieces and she's babbling like an idiot. "Please believe me. You can't think that I would…He was a monster. I'm…don't—I'm sorry."

Oriana reaches out for her again and cups her cheek. Her palm is hot, and Andy feels that same burn from before. It's magic.

"How long have you known Christian?"

The words are out before she can think. "I just met him. He was a friend of Dad's."

"Did you know he was the one who captured me?"

"Not at first. Once I realized who he was, I planned to kill him."

Another hand touches her shoulder. She's vaguely aware that the female angel has approached. Her hand does the same weird burning thing as Oriana's.

Faith shouts.

Josiah shouts.

The others start arguing.

Andy keeps staring at Oriana.

"Why were you with him?" asks Oriana.

"He called Dad's phone to tell him he'd found the demon."

"Why did you let him help you?"

"I told you." Her hands are shaking. "He blackmailed me."

"How did you find out he owned me?"

"He had one of your feathers." Her voice cracks. "It was black. They're so rare. I wasn't sure, but I thought it was yours." She's crying again. She's cried more lately than she's ever cried in her entire life. Fuck it. Humiliating or not, Oriana needs answers and she needs to know they're true.

"What was your plan?" asks Oriana.

"I was going to use him to distract the demon. I was going to let him fight it while I figured out how to restrain it."

"And?"

"And then I was going to kill him if the demon didn't and bring Mom back to see if Faith could save her."

"What happened?"

"He already knew that I knew you. He left me out there to die."

"That's why he told people you were dead?"

"Yeah. He thought the demon killed me."

"How did you survive?"

Andy closes her eyes and slams her mouth shut. That's Faith's business.

"Answer me."

She feels another burn deep in her chest. She can't stop herself. "Rescued," she chokes. "Faith." Her whole body is trembling. "Ana, please. I'm so sorry—for everything. I was a dick, I know, but I'd never…" Never what? Work with someone who was obviously demented? Deliberately torture living things just because? Betray Oriana?

She'd done all those things. It was all true. Oriana had every right to be angry. In fact, this is the way Oriana should have treated her from the beginning. Oriana was finally being smart about it.

"Can't trust me. I'm a liar. I hurt people. I didn't kill Christian because I'm so fucking numb, I didn't care what happened. I'm bad. You know that." Tears are flowing shamefully uninhibited down her face. She opens her eyes and all she can see is Oriana. "I'm a monster. I'll just hurt you again. I hurt everyone. I should have died so many times. I don't know why I'm alive. I'm not worth it. I shouldn't be here."

Oriana is so good and so strong. She's come so far—too far to be broken again by Andy. Oriana's hand falls away from Andy's cheek and the other angel releases her as well.

Andy crumples. She hides her face in her hands. She can feel everyone looking at her. They all heard. They all watched her break. She's back to reality. They all know the truth. "I'm sorry," she whispers. "I'm so fucking sorry."

Someone wraps their arms around her. Someone else is shouting. Someone pulls her up and pulls her away.

Ava and Tristan are shouting at the angels. Josiah and the woman are shielding Oriana behind their wings. Oriana is staring past them all, watching Andy.

Faith pulls Andy up to the house. "We couldn't get you away from them," she says. "I'm sorry. Josiah is strong. We couldn't get to you. That fucker. After all we've done. Are you all right?"

Andy wriggles free from Faith. "I'm okay," she says. "Don't be mad. They didn't do anything wrong. Oriana needed to hear that. Maybe she'll finally get it."

Faith grabs her by both shoulders and spins her around. "You are not bad," she says. "Understand? Bad shit happened, but *you* are not bad."

Andy sighs because her sister is still so innocent after all the shit she's seen. She'll always think the best of Andy, true or not.

The door opens and slams shut. Ava and Tristan storm inside.

"We got rid of them," says Tristan. "That was a complete violation."

"She didn't do anything wrong," says Andy.

"She attacked you," snaps Tristan.

"She was just trying to get me to talk."

"She was hurting you," says Ava. She's got a shotgun in her hands and Andy has no idea where it came from.

"She wanted to make sure I was telling the truth. I've been compelled by an angel before. She didn't do anything wrong."

"That was insanely intrusive," says Tristan.

"She thought I was friends with her fucking abductor," snaps Andy. "She needed to know the truth and she needed to be able to trust what I told her. If she has to use magic to figure out what's true, that's fine with me."

"This isn't a healthy relationship," says Tristan.

"I know! That's what I've been trying to tell you."

"It's not healthy for *you*, idiot."

"I think horrible things all on my own, thank you very much."

There is a timid knock at the door followed by a much louder banging. "It's Josiah! Don't shoot."

CHAPTER TWENTY-FIVE

Ava throws open the door and aims her shotgun at them. Oriana and the other angels are crowded around the door. Andy pushes past Faith and positions herself behind Ava. Oriana's face is twisted with an expression Andy's never seen on her.

"Oriana would like to speak to the trapper," says the female angel. "I think it's best if they speak alone. We can get acquainted elsewhere."

"Like hell," says Faith.

Oriana should have stayed away. Why did she come back? She's with other angels. She's safe now. They're clearly good at protecting her.

"Ms. Black," says the female angel, "they have unfinished business. I think our presence is causing them undue stress. If what Andy said is true, they deserve a chance to talk."

"Ava, move. It's just Oriana. She's not going to hurt us and she won't let these people hurt us."

"She just cast on you not fifteen minutes ago," says Ava.

"She compelled me. It's harmless. Move. I need to talk to Ana alone."

"Fine. You two can stay right here in the living room and we'll wait on the porch." She doesn't release her gun. "Andy, holler if you need us."

"Thank you. My name is Ariel. I'm sorry we didn't have a chance to make a formal introduction."

Oriana pushes past the other angels. Andy shoves Faith and Tristan outside. Their respective teams are still arguing when they shut the door.

Oriana looks up at Andy through long, dark lashes. "Forgive me. I thought—"

"You don't need to apologize. I get it."

"Are you hurt?" Oriana tilts her head, inspecting Andy.

"No, not at all."

"I've never seen you so upset."

Andy's cheeks are still burning from her tears. Her eyes are dry. She probably looks like shit. She rubs the back of her neck. "Yeah, that's been happening a lot lately."

"I didn't injure you?"

"No, I'm fine. I'm sorry I left you here. I'm sorry I said that stupid shit. I just—I wanted to make sure you knew what you were getting into with me."

"I think I have a better idea of it now," says Oriana. She takes a cautious step forward and Andy takes a step back. Then Oriana takes another step.

Andy holds her ground. "What are you doing?"

"I intend to make physical contact with you. Is that all right?"

"Yeah." She clenches her fists at her sides.

Oriana is only a few feet away. "You seem extremely uncomfortable."

"You've made a lot of progress. I don't want to be the thing that sets you back."

"You are not responsible for my setbacks." She takes another step, one hand extended and touches Andy's hand.

It's terrible and wonderful all at once. Andy can't focus on her thoughts as they fly through her mind, but she recognizes panic. What if this doesn't last? What if she's not good enough? What if she loves Oriana and Oriana doesn't love her? What if

Oriana loves her but she doesn't love Oriana? What if this is all for nothing? Does she love Oriana?

Oriana closes the space between them and takes Andy's face in her hands. Andy tries to relax. She rests her hands on Oriana's waist.

"I like your shirt," says Andy.

"Do not attempt to trivialize this moment."

"I wasn't—"

"Please."

The breath of the word ghosts over Andy's lips. She shuts up and Oriana kisses her. It's sweet and soft and it feels like absolution for her sins and Andy can feel another breakdown coming. Does she love Oriana or does she just love the way Oriana makes her feel? Does she need her or does she love her? Is she using Oriana so she can heal? Is she using her family?

"Andy," murmurs Oriana. She pulls away just enough to speak. "Your heart rate indicates you are uneasy."

"I'm not—"

Oriana silences her with a kiss to the cheek. She takes Andy's hand and leads them to the couch. She settles down beside Andy and spreads her wings to cocoon them in soft dark feathers.

"I am sorry I lost confidence in you," says Oriana.

"I'm sorry I diminished your decisions by assuming I know what's best for you." She can hear and feel it when Oriana laughs.

"You talked to Tristan."

"Faith *and* Tristan. And Ava—but you don't really talk to Ava so much as sit and listen while she lectures you about being a dumbass."

Oriana laughs again. "Your family gives good advice. I believe the angels were more interested in the dramatic nature of our relationship than a productive resolution."

"You told the angels about us?"

"Yes. I told them many things. I did try to keep our relationship secret at first. I think I missed you."

Andy pulls Oriana into her arms and nuzzles into her hair. "I missed you too. I shouldn't have run away."

"You panicked. I understand. I panicked too. I should have been more understanding of the depths of your self-worth issues."

"I don't—well, you have self-worth issues too."

"Yes, I am damaged and so are you. Perhaps that will result in a tempestuous relationship, but I am willing to try if you are."

"What if I hurt you?"

"Andy, we have two doctors, a retired trapper, and four angels watching us. I don't think we will be able to inflict any kind of irreparable damage."

"Four angels?"

"There are two more you haven't met."

Andy rests her head against Oriana, breathing in the scent of her hair. She sighs. "Yeah. You're the best thing to happen to me in a long fucking time."

"As Tabbris says, 'ditto.'"

"Who is Tabbris?"

"An angel. It's a long story." She doesn't get a chance to elaborate because someone knocks on the window.

Oriana unfolds her wings and they see Josiah's face pressed against the glass. "Can we come back in yet?" shouts Josiah.

"Yes," Oriana answers. She sighs. "Josiah is an acquired taste. But I think you will enjoy his use of sarcasm."

Josiah is the first one through the door. The others fall in behind him. "So you guys kissed and made up? I mean, we all watched you kiss and you're cuddling on the couch like teenagers, so I assume you made up."

"We've made up," says Oriana.

"Good," says Josiah. "We made up too."

Ariel and Josiah agree to stay the night.

Andy is relieved her family is together again.

Oriana is laying against Andy's chest with one wing draped over the side of the bed. Andy's itching to run her fingers through those soft black feathers, but she knows she should ask before she does it and she's not brave enough to broach the subject. She still can't shake the novelty of having an angel on top of her.

"You're sure you're comfortable?" asks Andy.

"Yes."

"Because I promise I won't take it personally if you don't want to stay with me."

"Do you want me to leave?"

"No," answers Andy quickly, "of course not."

"Then please shut up."

Andy laughs. "All right. Message received."

She is running her fingers over Andy's skin, leaving a little trail of heat as she moves.

This is right. She's home, the people she loves are safe, the woman she loves might just love her back. This is the best her life has ever been. It won't last, though. Oriana is an angel, and she needs to be with other angels. She's strong and smart and beautiful, and she finally seems to realize it.

Andy's human. How long can she possibly keep Oriana satisfied? "How long will you stay?" She knows as soon as Oriana gives her an answer she's going to start counting down the minutes until she leaves.

"I don't know. The angels are training me to become a guardian. I will need to return to them eventually."

Eventually.

Andy can't count down the minutes until "eventually" arrives.

"What's a guardian?"

"Someone who protects a designated territory. I am learning quickly. I will never be as strong as a true angel, but Ariel thinks I could be strong enough to be a guardian. I was thinking, once my training is complete, I could be the guardian for this region."

Andy hugs Oriana because, thank God. That's not what Andy thought she was going to say. "Yes! Do that. You could live here. You know, if you want to live here. Or we could get a place somewhere. Not that you have to move in with me."

Oriana puts her hand over Andy's mouth to shut her up. Andy is both amused and offended.

"What do *you* want?" she asks, taking her hand away from Andy's mouth.

That should be an easy question. "I don't know. Whatever you want."

"You can express your desire. I am not going to alter my wishes just to make them align with yours."

"I want you to stay here forever," says Andy, because why not go all in at this point? "Screw training. Just stay."

"No," says Oriana. She looks up and Andy looks away. "I do not want to 'screw training.' I want to learn more and visit you frequently until I am more competent with my power."

Andy risks looking down at her. That's reasonable. Oriana isn't leaving forever. She's just splitting her time. It's a healthy move for her. She needs to be around other angels.

"You can't manipulate me. You have no power. You impact me because I care about you, but that does not mean I will always bend to your wishes. Please stop worrying about it."

She is so strong.

Andy nods. "Okay. I trust you."

"I trust you, too."

"You better. It's pretty hard to lie to you since you can compel me."

She wilts back into Andy's chest. "I should not have used that on you."

Andy runs her fingers through Oriana's hair. "Don't worry about it. We can hate ourselves in the morning. Tonight, I just want to be happy that you came back."

"Agreed, but we still have a number of unpleasant things to discuss."

Andy tries not to wince. "Like what?"

"Like what happened when you encountered your mother, how you feel about trapping, the fact that I am not the only one of my kind, if your family's work has been compromised—"

"Not the only one of your kind? Way to bury the lede. Did you meet another half-angel?"

"No. Ariel told me there are others, or there *were* others. We are called hybrids and apparently, we are something of an atrocity in both realms."

"You're not an atrocity."

She shifts her wing, and her feathers puff up as they brush against Andy's body. "I believe you have a biased opinion."

"A psychopath and an atrocity. What a fucked-up pair we make."

She tilts her head up and kisses Andy's throat. "Come with me," she says. She folds her wing and gets up, dragging Andy out of bed.

"Where are we going?"

"It's a surprise." She pauses and frowns. "If this frightens you, please tell me and I will stop."

"Should I be worried?"

"No, this is perfectly safe, in theory. Though, admittedly, I've never tried it before." Oriana is leading them out of the house.

"Is this like an angel thing?"

"Something like that."

Andy follows her into the yard. Oriana spreads her wings and Andy's blood runs cold. It seems Oriana has already figured out that Andy's nervous. The angel pulls her into her arms. "Andy, this is meant to relax you."

"I'm relaxed."

Oriana is going to ask her to fly. She can do recreational flying, if it makes Oriana happy.

"You are clinging to me, and we have not even left the ground."

Whatever small hope Andy had that they were going to stay put is gone now. "Shit," she mutters. "Okay, we're going to fly. Right? That's why we're out here?"

Oriana kisses her and Andy forgets what she was talking about. "You do not have to fly with me if you don't want to."

"I want to but I just need to panic about it for a second."

"That seems counterproductive."

"Don't knock my method," says Andy. She rests her forehead against Oriana's shoulder.

She'd said she trusted her. They both said it. Was it true? Did Andy mean it? She feels Oriana squeeze her gently, pulling her closer. Yeah, she meant it. She trusts Oriana. She won't let them fall, but if she did let them fall, the impact would probably kill Andy and that might be for the best.

She shakes her head. She's spiraling.

Enough.

She's got to get away from herself. Maybe Oriana is right. "Okay, so, how are we going to do this? Is it like a hobbit/eagle situation or like a Lois Lane/Superman situation?"

"I will carry you, like this," answers Oriana, lifting Andy into her arms. "You will hold on—ouch—yes, like that."

"Sorry." She tries to relax her grip around Oriana's neck. She's not sure if her body responds to the command.

Oriana is still talking logistics. Andy nods along with her until she catches something about "another time" and realizes Oriana is offering her an out. "If I think about it any longer, I'm going to chicken out. Just go."

"Are you certain?"

"Just fly, Ana."

The instant those inky black wings twitch, Andy slams her eyes shut. The wind picks up. That's got to mean they're in the air. Oriana shifts Andy's body and she hangs on tighter. Has she always been this fragile? It's a miracle Jeremy ever let her get out of the car.

The wind slows and Oriana's body stills. It takes Andy a second to realize they're not falling. She risks opening an eye to make sure they're on the ground.

Oriana lowers Andy from her arms. "Are you all right?" she asks.

"I'm awesome. Just going to sit here on the ground for a second." Her knees do not support her like she thought they would, and she doesn't even bother trying to cover it when she collapses into the grass.

Wings brush against her and block out the world.

Oriana is sitting beside her. "Are you sure you're all right?"

"Yeah." She stares at the long black feathers. "I'm going to panic about it again for a few more seconds, then I want to give it another shot."

She remembers the first time Oriana sheltered her, when their funeral pyre erupted, and her wings kept Andy from getting burned. Oriana's wings would never fail her. She trusts them. She trusts Oriana. She takes her hand. "I'm ready. Let's try this again. Maybe I'll get brave and open my eyes."

"I won't drop you."

"I know." As soon as they're airborne Andy shuts her eyes.

The wind slows and Oriana shifts Andy in her arms. They're not on the ground, though. Andy can hear and feel Oriana's wings moving.

"We are hovering approximately fifteen feet above the ground. Do you want to get down?"

"No, I'm trying to be brave. I really want to look but I also really don't want to see how high we are."

"Most likely, a fall from this height would not hurt you."

"Gee, thanks."

She tries not to focus on the "most likely" part. For whatever reason, it works. Andy counts to three and then slowly opens her eyes.

Oriana is staring back at her.

"Hello, Andy," she says.

Andy grins. Oriana is patient and kind, completely in control, and she looks so damn pleased with herself.

"Hey, Ana," Andy says. She risks a quick glance down. "Okay, this isn't as terrible as I thought it was going to be."

Oriana is practically glowing. "Would you like to go higher?"

Andy doesn't miss the note of hope in her voice or the way the corner of her mouth twitches to conceal a smile. This is her world and she's sharing it with a human.

Andy nods. "Yeah, fuck it. Let's go higher."

CHAPTER TWENTY-SIX

Andy is selfish and doesn't regret it one damn bit. She monopolizes Oriana's time while she's at Ava's. Ariel doesn't visit much but Josiah likes to hang around. Faith and Tristan interview Josiah about angel culture.

Andy lets Oriana fly her up to the roof of the house. They can hear the others debating on the front porch.

"So wings don't really disappear," asks Faith, "they just shrink? How does that work? Can I see?"

"Sure," answers Josiah.

"Honey, he's fucking with you," says Tristan.

"How can you tell?" asks Faith.

Josiah starts snickering.

"That's how we can tell," answers Ava.

"You suck at this," says Josiah. "How are you a doctor?"

"My patients don't lie."

"How would you know?"

Andy doesn't need to see them to know Faith is pouting.

Oriana leans against her shoulder. One wing is curled around Andy, a habit that is quickly becoming the norm for them. Every time she feels feathers brush against her arm, Andy tries not to think about how much she's going to miss them when Oriana leaves.

Without warning, Oriana wraps her other wing around them and takes Andy's hand. She leads Andy's fingers to brush against the soft feathers at the arch of her wing.

Andy lets Oriana control the movements, not daring to deviate from the pace or motion she establishes. She feels Oriana's hand trembling against her own. She's sure Oriana can feel how hard her heart is beating. Slowly, she leads Andy to touch a long, silky primary feather. Andy remembers to breathe, then lightly runs a fingertip against the feather.

Oriana pulls her own hand away, trailing down Andy's outstretched arm until her palm is resting against Andy's shoulder.

"I trust you," says Oriana.

"Okay," breathes Andy. Emboldened, she lets her whole hand rest against the feathers.

Oriana flinches and pulls her wing back slightly before tensing her shoulders and pushing her wing back into Andy's touch. She turns her head and presses her face into Andy's body. "I really do trust you."

Andy pets the soft, silken feathers. "I know you do."

Maybe it's not love that makes her want to dive into Oriana's soul and melt into her being. Maybe she needs Oriana because she can't be alone—because she's afraid to lose another person, no matter how significant. Maybe it's not love. Maybe Andy's just needy.

"I'm beginning to think stress is contagious," mutters Oriana.

"Sorry."

"I'm not sure you started it."

Andy leans her cheek against Oriana. "That's us in a nutshell—an endless loop of freak-outs and stress."

"I'm told it gets better."

"Who told you that?"

"Tristan." Oriana pushes her wing into Andy's touch.

Andy slips her fingers into the feathers, and they disappear into the blackness. They stay huddled together on the roof long after the others go back inside.

Josiah leaves in the morning and Oriana leaves almost exactly a day later. Andy wants to drown in whiskey but doesn't because liquor is a poor substitute for her angel. Besides, Ava and Faith keep her too busy to drink. Faith finds ways to corner Andy into teaching impromptu angel anatomy lessons while Tristan always manages to appear as soon as the conversation begins. Ava decides Andy needs to learn how to fix a tractor, and she tows an ancient-looking machine out of the garage.

These activities occupy a grand total of two days and do very little to distract from the constant pounding of *Oriana, Oriana, Oriana* in Andy's thoughts.

On the third day, Faith and Tristan announce they will be leaving soon.

Everyone leaves.

Andy tries to be as rational about it as she can. They can't all live at Ava's forever. Faith has a life, a home, and patients who need her to come back. At some point, Andy will have to make a life for herself too. She tries not to think about all the skills she doesn't have or all the ways she does not fit in with the world. Instead, she spends her last few nights with Faith playing cards and sharing what she knows about angels and demons.

It's well after midnight when they finally call it a day. Andy heads up to her room. She's tired but doesn't expect to sleep. Oriana found a calling. She's going to be a guardian. She's going to have purpose. Faith and Tristan found a calling. They save lives. They fill a void in the world. Ava found a way to make the change from trapper to healer. The network trusts her, and Faith and Tristan need her.

Andy sits on the edge of her bed. She fits in here because her family has made a place for her. Jeremy made a place for her, too. Andy's not sure she's ever made a place for herself. She's not sure she knows how.

She drops her head into her hands and tries to find that quiet place in her head that helps her feel numb. Suddenly something warm wraps around her and two arms pull her close. Andy doesn't open her eyes. She breathes in the scent of honey and rain and surrenders to it. She melts into Oriana's body and rests her forehead on the angel's shoulder.

"You came back," mutters Andy.

"I said I would. I didn't realize you doubted me."

Andy starts to protest, but Oriana is faster.

"Don't bother denying it. Given your past and our somewhat tempestuous history, I suppose it's only natural for you to question my sincerity."

"Sorry."

"Don't be." Oriana closes her other wing around them and Andy can breathe again. "I thought you might not be here when I returned."

"Where else would I be?" Andy means to laugh but the sound loses its humor somewhere in the back of her throat. She changes the subject before Oriana can comment. "When did you get back?"

"Just a moment ago. I was going to wait until morning as to not wake the house, but I missed you."

"I missed you, too," says Andy.

"It's strange, longing to see someone after only being apart for a few days."

"It's endorphins or something." She inhales deeply, again filling her body with the scent of Oriana.

"It is not endorphins," she says.

Andy grins against the angel's skin. "I love you." Andy doesn't get the chance to panic or wonder if she said that loud enough for Oriana to hear.

"I love you, too."

Andy's chest tightens and she bites her lip. Somewhere in her mind a floodgate opened and now she's drowning. She clings to the angel. "My life doesn't have purpose," she whispers.

"Neither did mine, until a few weeks ago. Someone once told me life gets different and things can get better or worse in the blink of an eye."

Andy closes her eyes.

"You will find purpose," whispers Oriana, "but first you must heal. Rest for a few weeks and see if you feel better."

Andy laughs.

"Two weeks, to be specific," says Oriana.

"Yeah, I get it."

"I'm glad the irony of the situation is not lost on you."

Andy curls against her.

"I'm glad you shared that with me," she says.

"I didn't want to freak people out."

"Does your family know you've attempted to take your own life in the past?"

"No, or, I don't think so. I don't know. I try to keep them out of it but they always seem to know more than I think they do."

"Good. They should be aware of your state of mind."

"They don't need—"

"Yes, they do. They love you and if given the chance to share the burden of your suffering, I'm certain they would take it. You would do the same for them and you have done the same for me."

Andy wants to argue, but instead, just runs her fingers through Oriana's hair.

"You are the first person I've ever been in love with," says Oriana. "Do not take that away from me."

"I won't."

"Promise me."

"I promise."

"The world has a place for you. If there is a place for someone like me, I'm sure there is a place for someone like you." Oriana lifts her head and kisses Andy gently. "You saved my life, you know." She kisses Andy again. "You wrote to me in my language. You gave me the courage to hope someone could understand me." She kisses a spot just beneath Andy's ear. "You understood my pain enough to compromise with me. You recognized my autonomy." She pulls Andy's hand into her feathers. "You helped me fly. You wanted me to stay, but you let me go. You gave me my freedom."

"Ana, I—"

"You are a warrior, and if the humans won't have you, the angels will." She presses her wing into Andy's hand and kisses her deeply.

Andy feels something hot and powerful surge through her body. She can feel Oriana asking her to be quiet, to think and accept. She can feel it when Oriana whispers, "I love you," and she can feel her joy when Andy whispers it back.

She's not a trapper anymore but she is a warrior. They both are. There will always be battles to fight and souls to save. Their worlds need people who are too worn down to break, too numb to be hurt and too tainted to repent. They thrive in brutality and when their worlds cannot offer them comfort, they can find it with each other.

I love you.

Andy's not sure if she's thinking it on her own or feeling it from Oriana. It doesn't matter. She's sure they're thinking the same thing.

Bella Books, Inc.
Women. Books. Even Better Together.
P.O. Box 10543
Tallahassee, FL 32302
Phone: (800) 729-4992
www.BellaBooks.com

More Titles from Bella Books

Mabel and Everything After – Hannah Safren
978-1-64247-390-2 | 274 pgs | paperback: $17.95 | eBook: $9.99
A law student and a wannabe brewery owner find that the path to a
fairy tale happily-ever-after is often the long and scenic route.

To Be With You – TJ O'Shea
978-1-64247-419-0 | 348 pgs | paperback: $19.95 | eBook: $9.99
Sometimes the choice is between loving safely or loving bravely.

I Dare You to Love Me – Lori G. Matthews
978-1-64247-389-6 | 292 pgs | paperback: $18.95 | eBook: $9.99
An enemy-to-lovers romance about daring to follow your heart, even
when it's the hardest thing to do.

The Lady Adventurers Club - Karen Frost
978-1-64247-414-5 | 300 pgs | paperback: $18.95 | eBook: $9.99
Four women. One undiscovered Egyptian tomb. One (maybe) angry
Egyptian goddess. What could possibly go wrong?

Golden Hour - Kat Jackson
978-1-64247-397-1 | 250 pgs | paperback: $17.95 | eBook: $9.99
Life would be so much easier if Lina were afraid of something
basic—like spiders—instead of something significant. Something like
real, true, healthy love.

Schuss – E. J. Noyes
978-1-64247-430-5 | 276 pgs | paperback: $17.95 | eBook: $9.99
They're best friends who both want something more, but what if
admitting it ruins the best friendship either of them have had?